Cash wrenched his mouth from hers and they stared at each other in stunned silence, their chests heaving, breathing ragged.

Lucy couldn't tear her gaze away from Cash's.

He didn't look like a guy who was acting.

He looked as smitten as she was.

'You'd do anything for the cameras,' she said, eager to break the unbearable tension between them.

He ducked his head to whisper in her ear. 'If that was you playacting, sweetheart, I'll double your fee.'

She tossed her head. 'Okay. So we kissed. Big deal.'

'We're attracted to each other.' He ran a fingertip down her cheek. 'It's not a crime to admit it.'

Lucy gritted her teeth. No way could she admit to wanting Cash.

The last thing she needed was to get involved in some weird half-assed relationship that had started out fake and yet involved very real sex.

Sex? Yikes. She really was in trouble.

Dear Reader

Valentine's Day can inspire mixed feelings in people.

If you're part of a romantic couple the pressure's on for your better half to impress with grand gestures.

If you're single you harbour hopes that a secret admirer will finally declare his undying love while trying not to turn a pale shade of green as your BFF's partner lavishes her with gifts and flowers.

For confirmed romance cynics like Lucy and Cash, Valentine's Day can be summed up in a few words: over-commercialised claptrap for gullible fools!

So what happens when these two cynics must fake a relationship for a week in the lead-up to the big day?

Will true love win over the most hardened hearts?

I had so much fun having Lucy and Cash deal with a variety of romantic situations designed to taunt and challenge.

The outcome?

This confirmed romantic is not telling.

You'll need to read the book to find out!

Happy reading!

Nicola

www.nicolamarsh.com

ROMANCE FOR CYNICS

BY
NICOLA MARSH

8000 000 011 1417

Published in Great Britain 2014
by Mills & Boon, an imprint of Harlequin (UK) Limited,
Eton House, 18-24 Paradise Road, Richmond, Surrey, TW9 1SR

© 2014 Nicola Marsh

ISBN: 978 0 263 24175 4

Printed and bound in Great Britain
by CPI Antony Rowe, Chippenham, Wiltshire

Nicola Marsh has always had a passion for writing and reading. As a youngster she devoured books when she should have been sleeping, and later kept a diary whose contents could be an epic in itself!

These days, when she's not enjoying life with her husband and sons in her home city of Melbourne, she's at her computer, creating the romances she loves in her dream job.

Visit Nicola's website at www.nicolamarsh.com for the latest news of her books.

This and other titles by Nicola Marsh
are available in eBook format
at www.millsandboon.co.uk

This one is for my dedicated readers and fellow romantics who believe true love will always triumph.

May all your happily-ever-afters be a heartbeat away.

CHAPTER ONE

'THIS IS A screw-up of monumental proportions.' Cashel Burgess flung the daily newspaper on his desk and glared at the offending print.

Maybe if he stared at it hard enough this whole damn mess would disappear.

As if.

'That'll teach you for dating beautiful bimbos.' Barton Clegg, an old college buddy who had the power to get him out of this godforsaken mess, pointed at the picture in the paper. 'She's a stunner all right, but Cash?' Barton made a gesture resembling grabbing him by the balls and twisting. 'She's got you by these, mate.'

'Tell me something I don't know.' Cash pushed away from his desk, stood and resumed pacing, something he'd been doing way too much of since he'd learned the starlet he'd given financial advice to over a long lunch was concocting some twisted version of what had happened between the veal scaloppini and tiramisu.

'Why did you call me over?'

'Damage control.' Cash stopped pacing and stabbed a finger at the paper. 'You know I lost a packet when that overseas bank went under. And now this. If I lose clients over some slighted woman's concocted BS...' Cash shook his head. 'The PR firm you work for is the best in the business. I need you to boost my profile to over-shadow this crap.'

He turned the newspaper over before he did some-thing crazy. Like stab a letter opener through the woman's heart.

Bart shook his head. 'We're not taking on new clients at the moment, you know that.'

Cash frowned and stared down his soon-to-be former best friend. 'You owe me after I got your ass out of trou-ble the night the dean bailed you up following that butt-out-the-back-window-of-the-uni-bus prank.'

Bart grinned like a goofball. 'Those were the days.'

Cash rolled his eyes. 'You're a putz.'

'A putz that's going to get you out of a fix, apparently.' Bart swivelled on the ergonomic chair. 'I can put in a good word for you but it won't do any good...'

A frown momentarily creased Bart's brow before he snapped his fingers and leaped from the chair. 'There is a way the firm can take you on. Guaranteed.'

Relieved he'd found a way out of this mess, Cash nod-ded. 'Whatever it is, I'll do it.'

A knowing grin spread across his friend's face. 'Sure?'

Pinching the bridge of his nose, Cash perched on the edge of his desk. 'As you so delicately implied, that woman has my balls in a vice, so yeah, I'll do anything.'

'Fine. Then all you need to do is find yourself a girl-friend for a week.'

'What the—?'

'The firm's running a massive fundraiser in the lead up to Valentine's Day. A week-long love-in, where cou-ples do a bunch of mushy stuff together, get filmed, soundbites get posted on the firm's website and peo-ple vote for the most romantic couple.' Bart's smug grin widened. 'You wanted positive PR. What could be better than raising a stack of cash for a good cause while being viewed by millions? Oh, and make sure your *girlfriend* is clean and wholesome, the opposite of your usual arm candy.'

Speechless, Cash gaped at his friend. 'Are you freaking crazy? Where the hell do I find a girlfriend for a week?'

Bart waved away his concern. 'Minor details.' He strolled towards the massive French windows overlooking the sprawling lawn of Cash's Williamstown mansion. 'I'm sure you'll figure something out.'

Cash's fingers curled into fists. This couldn't be happening. Bad enough he'd lost a bundle after following a bad investment tip from one of the best in the business, an old college mentor.

But having some scorned woman spreading gossip and innuendo about him because he'd knocked her back? That was something else. She was damaging his reputation in an industry where reputation was everything.

He gave financial advice to the stars. Australia's elite actors and musicians came to him when they wanted to invest their money. And he'd built a considerable fortune from it.

He liked money. Liked the comfort derived from seeing cold, hard cash accumulate in the bank, providing security and reliability. Two things he'd never had growing up.

With the threat of his cash source drying up, Cash had turned to Bart. His mate's solution sounded easy enough but he couldn't exactly pull a girlfriend out of thin air.

Bart wolf-whistled. 'Hey, what about her?'

'Who?'

'The hottie in the obscenely tight shorts.'

Cash crossed to the window, where Bart had his nosed pressed against the glass like a hormonal teenager.

'Lucy? You're kidding, right?'

Lucy Grant, his gardener, would be the last woman he'd ask to be his fake girlfriend for a week.

The woman despised him.

Not that she'd ever said or done anything overt, but she gave off an air of untouchability that made him want to ruffle her.

So he'd tried. Several times. Whenever they crossed paths, he'd flirt with her. Deliberately taunting, trying to get a rise out of her.

Nada.

Her hands-off aura intrigued him a little, but he hadn't given her aloofness much thought. Except those odd times he'd been taking a business call and found himself at this very window, copping a very nice eyeful of firm ass, long legs and B-cups in a tight tank top.

Watching Lucy stride as she mowed his lawn or bend over as she clipped hedges made working from home that much more pleasurable.

In fact, he timed his rare workdays from home with her fortnightly gardening visits. Maybe she'd crack one of these days and give him a smile? Doubtful, considering the death glare she'd shot him this morning when they'd crossed paths on the back patio.

'Why not?' Bart peeled his nose away from the window with reluctance. 'The firm only has room for one more couple and they're closing applications today.' He tapped the side of his nose. 'I put in a good word for you and you're in. Guaranteed.'

'You're nuts,' Cash said, his gaze unwittingly drifting to where Lucy stood near the front gate, pruning with her usual efficiency.

For all he knew, Lucy had a hubby and a string of dirt-smudged rug-rats at home. Though she didn't wear a ring...not that it meant anything. Probably took it off for safety reasons while working.

Cash shook his head. 'I don't know the woman.'

'No time like the present to get to know her.' Bart glanced at his watch. 'I need to head back to the office and I need your answer now. You in?'

Tension knotted the muscles in Cash's neck. The last thing he felt like doing was parade around for seven days acting like a lovestruck fool.

But his business was everything. He'd worked too long and too hard to let it suffer because of circumstances beyond his control.

He'd approached Bart because he needed positive PR. But Valentine's Day? Seriously?

'Three...two...one...' Bart made a buzzing sound and Cash nodded.

'Fine. I'll do it.'

Bart smirked as he shrugged into his suit jacket. 'So who's the lucky lady going to be?'

'Leave that to me,' Cash said, mentally scrolling through his list of female friends and coming up empty.

Half of them he'd dated and would never go there again. The other half wanted more and would see this week of lovey-dovey crap as a full-blown declaration.

Uh-uh. He needed someone without any romantic illusions.

Someone without any view to the future.

Someone without cunning, ulterior motives or the urge to shackle him to a ball and chain.

As he walked Bart out and Lucy acknowledged him with a curt nod, he knew.

He needed someone like Lucy.

* * *

'Damn it.' Lucy's pruning shears slipped and she hacked off a chunk of ivy leaf violet when Cash appeared at the front door.

The guy had that effect on her. The ability to raise her hackles and make her want to chop something off—not of the flora variety.

Not his fault entirely, that she had a healthy disregard for millionaires in slick suits. It was a personal aversion, one she'd honed to a fine art nine years ago.

And Cash seemed more charming than most, with his ready smile and quick wit. But that was what put her on guard: his ability to flirt without trying, his easy-going approach when she knew it would be a practiced façade presented to the world.

Go-getters like him wouldn't get anywhere if they were that laid-back all the time. And she knew enough about her number one client Cashel Burgess, courtesy of Google, to assume he would be a tiger in the boardroom.

Self-made millionaire by the time he was twenty-eight. High IQ, skipped a year at high school. Economics degree. MBA. Impressive jobs at elite actuary firms before opening his own financial advisory business to the stars.

He moved in A-list circles, often gracing the social pages and gossip columns in Melbourne media. Par for the course, considering he always had a busty blonde actress on his arm. She half expected to see the entire female cast of Melbourne's top-rating soap opera stroll out of his house the mornings she worked here, but surprisingly she'd never seen a woman do the walk of shame out of his enviable mansion. Perhaps he spirited them away out the back.

No, she didn't trust guys who behaved one way in public and another in private. Which was why she preferred ignoring him when they crossed paths every two weeks.

She knew her aloofness was why he deliberately went out of his way to seek her out. He saw her coolness as a challenge. She didn't let it bother her. If anything, she notched her haughtiness up further. No way in hell would she ever let down her guard, because then she might have to face reality: that a small part of her was super attracted to the whole casually mussed brown hair, piercing blue eyes, chiselled jaw, dimpled smile thing he had going on.

Unfathomable. And wrong on so many levels, considering she'd vowed to never go for a suit again.

Must be her dating drought making her secretly lust after her boss. Maybe she should say yes the next time the guy at the hardware shop asked her out?

Cash's visitor slid into a Porsche and backed out of the drive with a jaunty wave in her direction. She managed a terse nod in response and gripped the pruning shears, ready to resume work.

However, rather than heading back into the house, Cash started down the path towards her.

Crap.

They'd already done their usual him-flirt-her-avoid dance this morning so what did he want now? An encore?

She opened the shears then snapped them shut with a loud metallic clink that carried clear across the garden and she could've sworn she saw Cash falter, wince or both. Probably wishful thinking but she did it again for good measure.

'Is that a warning?' he said, eyeing the shears with a mix of wariness and amusement.

The corners of her mouth twitched against her better judgement. 'No, but it could be if you keep hassling me while I'm trying to work.'

He smiled and the impact of those lips curving hit her somewhere in the vicinity of her solar plexus. 'Why don't you put the DIY castrating tool down so we can talk?'

This time, she couldn't stop the laughter spilling from her lips. 'About?'

'Wow.' He clutched his heart and staggered a little. 'You're gorgeous when you smile.'

'And you're full of it.' She waved the shears in his direction. 'What do you want?'

He flinched. 'Not that.'

Damn, she loved sparring with a quick-witted guy. And if she were completely honest with herself, she missed it. Missed the fun of swapping banter with a guy who could fire back.

'I'm busy—'

'I really need to talk to you.' His sincerity scared her as much as his overt flirting. 'Would you like to come inside for a drink?'

'No thanks.' She shook her head. Bad enough bumping into him outside. No way would she set foot inside his place and risk pining for what she'd once had.

She'd put her past behind her a long time ago but she'd be lying if she didn't admit there were times when she missed the luxury, the wealth, the glamour. 'What's up? Is it my work—?'

'No, nothing like that.' He huffed out a breath and for the first time since she'd started working for the tycoon six months ago via referral, he appeared uncertain and unsure. And damn, if that hint of vulnerability didn't make him all the more appealing.

'I have a problem I need your help with.' A frown appeared between his brows. 'Actually, it's more than a problem. More like an impending catastrophe.'

Her curiosity was piqued. 'Unless it has something to

do with your jasmine wilting or your compost needing mulching, not sure what I can do to help.'

His frown eased as his mouth lost its pinched quirk. 'This isn't a gardening matter.'

'Then I'm not sure what I can do—'

'I need a fake girlfriend for a week and you'd be perfect.'

CHAPTER TWO

THE SHEARS SLIPPED from Lucy's hand and clattered to the path, thankfully missing her steel-capped boots, which had cost a small fortune.

She stared at Cash in disbelief. 'You're crazy—'

'Just hear me out, okay?' He held up his hands. Yeah, as if that would stop her from knocking some sense into him. Figured. The smart, gorgeous, funny ones were always certified lunatics.

'My business is in danger of losing some major clients and I need a mega-positive PR injection.' He pressed his temple, as if staving off a headache. She knew the feeling. 'GR8 4U Public Relations is the best in Melbourne and they're running a week-long fundraiser, which would be perfect for my business's needs, but the catch is I need to be part of a couple.' He nodded at her. 'And that's where you come in.'

She laughed, great hysterical peals she couldn't stop once she started.

'It's not that funny,' he said, eyeing her with a beguiling blend of wounded pride and little-boy-lost.

'It's freaking hilarious.' She clutched her sides and huddled over a little, drawing in deep breaths to stop the giggles. 'You've probably got a host of bimbos on speed dial and you think *I* should be your fake girlfriend?'

The chuckles started again and she would've had a hard time stopping them if Cash hadn't placed a finger against her lips to quiet her.

As a silencing technique, it worked a treat. Because the moment he touched her, laughter was the furthest thing from her mind, considering she had to muster indignation or annoyance or *something* to stop from doing what she'd like to: kiss that finger.

She swatted his hand away and he continued. 'All the women I know would be unsuitable. They want a commitment or a wedding ring. That's why you'd be perfect.'

As she opened her mouth to argue he said, 'You don't like me.'

'That's the first sensible thing you've said all day.'

His eyes narrowed. 'Believe me, if I had other options I'd take them but my business is everything to me and I can't afford to lose it.'

'With a place like this, surely you've got a few million or ten stashed away for a rainy day?' She gestured at the house, a two-storey French Provincial style mansion sprawled across a double block on Williamstown's foreshore, where real estate prices were sky-high. 'Why don't you dip into that?'

His lips compressed into a thin, angry line. 'I need the positive PR more than the money.'

If this wasn't about his business losing clients and money, there must be one hell of a good reason why he'd approached her, a woman he barely knew, to pose as his girlfriend for a week.

'Why?' She pinned him with the usual glare she reserved for their brief meetings. 'What aren't you telling me?'

His gaze shifted to stare over her shoulder, focused on the intense blue of Port Phillip Bay on a perfect summer's day. 'I work with famous people whose egos are as big as the pay cheques they want me to invest for them. My reputation is everything. And if that's tarnished in any way...'

She raised her eyebrows, encouraging him to continue. He shook his head and his pained expression almost made her feel sorry for him. Almost. 'One of Melbourne's hottest actresses didn't take too kindly to my refusing her offer of...uh, side benefits to our business arrangement.'

The unexpected jab of jealousy took her by surprise, as did the begrudging respect. Not many red-blooded guys would turn down taking things further with the sort of woman she knew Cash did business with.

'Anyway, she's spreading rumours. Bad ones. And I can't go on the record in the media without adding fuel to the fire and looking like a callous bastard, so I need to tackle this a different way.'

'And you think having a fake girlfriend for a week will do the trick?' She smothered her chuckle when he glared at her. 'Seriously, I need to get back to work—'

'There'll be a significant financial incentive.'

And just like that, Lucy's respect for the crazy yet gorgeous Cash plummeted. 'You want to *pay* me to be your girlfriend?'

He puffed up as if she'd insulted him. 'Well, there has to be something in it for you, right?'

His assessing gaze slid over her, leaving her skin prickling. 'It's not like you'd do it out of the goodness of your heart.'

She snapped her fingers. 'That's right, considering *I don't even like you.*'

Sick of the distraction, and ultimate stuff-up of her time management for the day, she picked up the shears. 'Don't worry, I'm sure you'll find some other poor sucker—uh, I mean eternally grateful, simpering female to pander to your every whim for a week.'

He folded his arms, unimpressed by her flippancy. 'So you won't do it?'

She snapped the shears twice in response.

'There's nothing I can give you to sweeten the offer?'

She didn't like the way her stomach fell at his smooth tone. 'Nope. Not a thing. Not even if you promised to walk through Melbourne in a pair of my shorts, or gave me carte blanche to remodel this entire garden from start to finish.'

Actually, she could be tempted by that. Not the shorts thing. The garden. It was something she'd thought about often while doing the basic maintenance.

A garden like this deserved to be loved and made to shine. Mowing the lawn and keeping the hedges trimmed was a travesty, considering the underlying beauty.

How many times had she mentally planned a complete redesign? Loads, because she liked to daydream while she worked. Liked to envisage her landscaping business gaining notoriety so she could work on some of the city's many beautiful gardens.

Ironic, that one of the things that mattered to her most these days—her job—was born from her disastrous marriage.

The sprawling garden surrounding Adrian's Toorak mansion had been incredible. She'd spent many hours there, first entertaining, later losing herself in tending to it to block out the ever-increasing evidence that her husband was a lying, cheating scumbag.

She'd buried herself in books too, doing a horticultural science course to foster her love of all things green, and by the time the divorce had come through Lucy's Landscaping had been a thriving business for a year.

She liked maintaining pristine gardens of the wealthy clients she'd once called friends. They trusted her and she ignored their pitying glances and overt condescension. Gardening paid the bills and made her happy. Nothing else mattered, apart from Gram, the woman who'd given her courage to leave Adrian in the first place.

Calculated interest sparked Cash's eyes. 'What if I said you could re-landscape the entire place?'

Damn her traitorous heart for leaping at the prospect. 'Do you know how much that would set you back?'

His lips curved. 'I'm sure you'll enlighten me.'

'Thirty grand.'

To his credit, he didn't blink. Typical millionaire.

'I need you as my girlfriend, Lucy,' he said, taking a step closer. Too close. The scent of his spicy shower gel mingling with the nearby Daphne to make her swoon a little. 'Please?'

With his big blue eyes fixed on her and that devastatingly sexy smile, Lucy wondered how many women had actually managed to say no to Cash Burgess.

She bet she'd be the first.

'Sorry, can't do it.' She made a grand show of glancing at her watch. 'And if you'll excuse me, I'm late for an appointment.'

Before he could respond, she tucked the pruning shears into the tool belt around her waist and pushed the lawnmower towards her trailer as fast as her legs could carry her.

Because for one tension-fraught second, with that silent plea in his steady gaze, she'd almost said yes.

Lucy had barely kicked off her boots at her grandmother's back door and entered the kitchen when she knew something was drastically wrong.

Gram baked every morning. If Lucy gardened to forget her husband, Gram baked to remember hers.

She supplied local cafés and schools and the local homeless shelter. Baking was Gram's thing. So to enter the kitchen Lucy had grown up in to find Gram sitting motionless at the dining table with a stack of documents spread before her? As unforeseeable as Cash's girlfriend-for-a-week proposal.

'Gram, what's wrong?' Lucy pulled up a chair next to her grandmother and reached for her hand, its icy clamminess making foreboding slither through her.

Gram shook her head, the tears trickling down her cheeks as terrifying as her dazed stare fixed on the documents.

Lucy reached for the top one, surprised when Gram's fingers clamped on her wrist and dug in with surprising strength.

'Don't.'

That one word held so much sorrow and pain and devastation, Lucy felt tears burn her eyes.

'Gram, please, you're scaring me—'

'I could lose everything,' Gram murmured, pushing the papers away so fast they scattered on the kitchen floor. 'I loved your grandfather but by goodness he was a selfish bastard.'

Lucy stared, shock rendering her incapable of speech. Gram had adored Pops, who'd died twelve months ago. And in all the years they'd raised her, she'd never heard Gram utter one bad word about him.

Lucy had been amazed at how well Gram had handled his death, how pragmatic she'd been. And while she'd seen Gram shed tears at the funeral and afterwards, she'd never seen her look so fiercely angry or blatantly upset.

Lucy laid a comforting hand on her shoulder. 'Tell me what's happened.'

Gram finally raised grief-stricken eyes to meet hers. 'I could lose the house.'

Lucy heard the five words but couldn't comprehend them. She'd lived most of her life in this house, since her parents had been killed in a car crash when she'd been a toddler.

This cosy cottage in Footscray, one of Melbourne's working-class suburbs, had been filled with love and laughter and food. Her friends had flocked once news of Gram's lamingtons and jam tarts and lemon slices had spread, and her grandparents enjoyed being surrounded by young people as much as she revelled in the attention of being smothered with love.

Gram had often told her the story of how Pops had surprised her with the house as a wedding present and Lucy loved the romance of it all. Probably why she'd fallen for her own version of Prince Charming, with Adrian whisking her to live in his palace after they'd married. Pity her prince turned into a toad. But Gram had lived here for almost fifty years. How could she lose the only home she'd ever known?

'I don't understand.' In fact, Lucy didn't understand much of what had happened today. Tears blurred Gram's eyes again and she blinked several times before continuing. 'I'd hoped to avoid telling you any of this, love, but I don't know who else to turn to.'

Lucy gripped Gram's hand tight. 'You're starting to really worry me, Gram. Tell me everything.'

Gram dragged in a breath and let it out slowly. 'Your grandfather had a gambling addiction. I didn't know 'til after he died and the debts started rolling in.'

For the second time in as many minutes, Lucy stared at Gram, dumbstruck.

'I paid off most of them from our life savings and his small superannuation payout, but now this...' She picked up the sole remaining document on the table. 'Your grandfather remortgaged the house to the tune of fifty thousand dollars. And unless I can start making repayments...'

Gram ended on a sob that galvanised Lucy into action. She wrapped her arms around Gram and hung on for dear life, letting her own tears fall. Tears of betrayal, of sadness, of disappointment.

Pops had been her idol. The kind of man she wished Adrian had been like. Moral. Upstanding. Dependable.

To discover it was all a lie was almost as devastating as learning the truth about Adrian's indiscretions.

When Gram's sobs petered out, Lucy gently disengaged. 'It's okay, Gram, I'll help.'

'I'm not taking money from you,' Gram said, her frown fierce. 'You've got your own mortgage and business. I won't have you running into financial troubles because of me.'

'Then we'll sell this place and you can live with me—'

'No. A young woman needs her independence and how will you find your own happiness with an old woman crowding your space?' Gram's mouth twisted in a mutinous grimace. 'I have my pride and I'm not leaving this house 'til I'm taken out in a wooden box.'

Lucy only just caught her added, 'Which may be my only option.'

The thought of Gram doing anything drastic chilled her blood and she grabbed Gram's upper arms and gave a little shake. 'I don't ever want to hear you talking like that. You're a fighter. You inspired me to fight for what was right with Adrian. You taught me how to survive upheaval and sadness.'

Lucy swallowed the huge lump of emotion clogging her throat. 'You're all I have left.'

Guilt clouded Gram's watery gaze. 'I'm sorry, love, that was a stupid thing to say. 'Course I'd never do anything silly.'

'You better not.' Lucy glared at her for good measure. 'So if you're too bloody stubborn to move in with me and you won't let me help pay your mortgage, what are we going to do?'

'Got a spare fifty grand lying around?' Gram joked, trying to alleviate the hopelessness of the situation.

And in that moment, Lucy remembered where she could get her hands on a sizable amount of cash, almost enough to clear Gram's debt and keep her house safe.

'Actually, I just might.'

Gram started, then waggled her finger. 'Don't you dare even think of approaching that no-good son-of-a-bitch ex-husband of yours to ask for the money.'

Lucy snorted. 'Gram, we're desperate, but not that desperate. It's been nine years since I've seen Adrian and I intend to keep it that way.'

'Good.' Gram tilted her head to one side, studying her. 'Then where are you going to get that kind of money?'

'I've got a plan,' Lucy said, with a sinking heart.

Sadly, it involved backtracking on her adamant stance to not be Cash Burgess's fake girlfriend for a week, and seeing if she could coerce him into throwing another twenty grand into the coffers to remodel his garden.

'Is it legal?'

'Barely,' Lucy said, with a wry grin.

'Luce...' She'd heard Gram's warning tone so many

times as a teenager, it made her feel gooey inside to hear it now.

'Gram, trust me. You'll be the first to know what's going on once I get everything sorted.'

'You're a good girl, Luce, always have been.' Gram patted her cheek. 'I just wish I could've preserved the memory of your grandfather for you.'

Touched by her grandmother's concern considering the betrayal she must be feeling, Lucy smiled. 'Nobody's perfect, Gram. Pops must've loved you, and me, very much to try and hide his addiction from us. Does it hurt? You bet. Was he selfish in dumping all this trouble on you? Absolutely. But nothing can taint how much he loved us.' She took a deep breath. 'He taught me so much. You both did, and I love you for it.'

Gram swiped at her eyes again. 'Damn waterworks. You've set me off again.'

Lucy sniffled. 'Dry your eyes. I have a hankering for your signature lemon tart when I return so start baking.'

'Where are you going?'

'To see a man about a plan.'

And a garden.

And a pact that would see her pose as Cash Burgess's girlfriend for a long seven days.

Desperate times indeed.

CHAPTER THREE

LUCY SPIED CASH sitting on the back patio the moment she rounded the side of the house.

He had a stack of manila folders scattered on the table, an open laptop and a mobile phone. But he wasn't working. Instead, he stared into space, a frown grooving his brows.

Gone was the *über*-confident air he wore like the finest designer suit. He looked like a guy with mega problems.

She knew the feeling.

Even now, thirty minutes later, she was still reeling from the news of her grandfather's gambling addiction.

Not once had she suspected he had a problem. He'd worked hard his entire life at the local paper-mill factory, had given her and Gram a secure home, food on the table and the occasional holiday to Sydney.

Hers hadn't been a Spartan upbringing but they hadn't been flush with cash either. She wondered later, after her marriage went pear-shaped, if that had been a major attraction with Adrian. Not that she married him for his money. In fact, she hadn't known the extent of his wealth until they'd been dating a few months and by then she was head over heels. But the money had been a welcome bonus after her frugal family life.

After he'd retired Pops had played lawn bowls, hung out at the pub with his mates to watch the horse racing on a Saturday arvo and gone into town weekly for lunch with his poker club.

Now, those outings took on a whole new meaning. Rather than having a beer with his cronies, he'd probably been gambling heavily, losing his hard-earned savings, then borrowing on the house he'd paid off years earlier.

Poor Gram. Lucy admired her resilience. And her pride. She didn't blame Gram for not wanting to move in with her. The small outer-city weatherboard house she'd bought after the divorce was cosy on a good day. She loved its quaintness and what the house lacked in size, the garden more than made up for.

It had been the major attraction when she'd been house hunting and she'd fallen in love with the English cottage garden gone wild and the massive veggie patch.

The house could've been a shack for all she cared once she'd seen the garden but, thankfully, the Californian-bungalow-styled house was perfect for her needs.

Having Gram sell her house and move in had seemed like the only option at the time when she'd heard of her grandfather's treachery.

But there was another solution to Gram's financial woes and Lucy was looking straight at him.

She bounded up the steps, intent on being friendlier. Because if Cash had found a replacement fake girlfriend in the last half-hour, she was screwed.

'Sorry to interrupt, but do you have a minute?'

He glanced at her hands and raised an eyebrow. 'No unspoken castration threats via gardening tools this time?'

'My idea of a joke,' she said, sitting in the wrought-iron

chair opposite without waiting to be asked. 'Probably a touch of sunstroke. Gardeners' occupational hazard.'

The corners of his mouth eased into a smile that slugged her to the gut. 'But it's cloudy today.'

She smiled at him in return. 'Can't you give a girl a break?'

'I will if you do that more often.' He leaned forward and traced her mouth, his fingertip doing crazy things to her insides.

Considering they had to fake it for the next week, her reaction to the charmer? Not good.

She leaned back, out of touching reach. 'Trust me, I'll be all smiles if I'm your girlfriend for the week.'

His eyebrows shot up so fast she laughed.

'Yeah, I changed my mind.' She held up a finger. 'With one stipulation. Your garden quote increases to fifty grand.'

His eyes narrowed in speculation. 'For that price I could hire every PR firm on the eastern seaboard to make me look good.'

'Yeah, but you wouldn't have an amazing garden at the end of it or have me on your arm playing the devoted girlfriend doing whatever I'm supposed to be doing.'

She made it sound like an offer too good to refuse when in fact she'd be getting a lot more out of this bizarre arrangement than him.

Payment for the garden refurbishment would clear Gram's debt and keep her cottage safe, while the huge boost to her profile in the landscaping business would ensure other wealthy clients would hire her. And that in turn would enable her to set up a healthy nest egg so Gram could see out her days in peace.

Gram deserved that safety net, after raising her.

He continued to study her, coolly assessing. 'What made you change your mind?'

'Would you believe a woman's prerogative?'

'No.'

'I need the money.' A half-truth that would have to suffice. She didn't know Cash Burgess—had no intention of getting to know him. Theirs was a mutually beneficial business arrangement. End of story.

The fact she was a teensy-weensy bit attracted to him? Irrelevant. Besides, she had little doubt that spending a week in his obnoxiously superior company would cure her of *that*.

After what felt like an eternity, where he seemed to study every freckle on her nose, he nodded. 'You pose as my girlfriend for a week. Attend a few PR functions. Boost my profile. No romantic entanglement whatsoever. And I'll pay you fifty grand to remodel my garden. Deal?'

He held out his hand and she shook it. 'Deal.'

But rather than let go of her hand, Cash held it firmly, tugged hard, and pulled her half across the table to meet his lips.

This was so not part of the plan.

Damn. Cash had wanted to rattle Lucy's customary cool exterior. Had wanted to see if he could get a reaction out of her other than a smart-ass comeback.

The impulsive kiss had been about making a dent in her impenetrable armour.

It hadn't been about making him want more, to the point where he could easily have devoured her.

He'd expected a rough shove away and a resounding slap. He hadn't expected her lips to soften, to mould, to cling.

And then she made a sound, a soft, seductive sigh that shot straight to his groin.

He wrenched his mouth from hers and stared in fascination at the woman who would be his girlfriend for a week.

Looked like faking it for the cameras with Lucy wouldn't be such a hardship after all.

'What was that all about?' She swiped the back of her hand across her mouth, as if she couldn't stand the thought of boy cooties.

'Seeing if we'd be compatible.'

She didn't like his smug, trite answer, her big brown eyes sparking caramel fire. 'Don't you dare do that again—'

'Can't promise that, considering we'll be hamming up the romance in front of the cameras.'

'Cameras?'

His grin widened. 'The firm who's doing me a favour, GR8 4U Public Relations, are filming the couples involved, posting snippets on the firm's website for voting, and the most voted couple raises the most funds for charity.'

'We're being filmed?' Horror darkened her eyes as she waved her hand between them. 'So you and I will need to…I mean, we'll have to act all lovey-dovey…bloody hell.'

He laughed. 'Don't worry. I'm not expecting to win the thing. Just being in the competition is going to provide all the positive publicity I need to stave off any damage that woman can possibly inflict.'

She cocked her head to one side, studying him. 'Can I ask you something?'

'Anything for my *girlfriend*.'

With an exasperated sigh, she ignored his wink.

'What if people don't buy our charade? Will you screw me over?'

After that surprisingly sizzling kiss, Cash wished Lucy wouldn't allude to him screwing her over anything.

He shook his head. 'Whatever the result of the Valentine's Day competition, you'll get your chance to tackle this garden and get your money.'

Her nose wrinkled as if she'd smelled something nasty. 'Valentine's Day?'

He could understand her dislike for the ridiculous day that made flower vendors a lot of money and idiots out of any self-respecting guy. 'We attend a week of romantic functions in the lead-up to Valentine's Day, where the winner is announced at a formal ball.'

'This just gets better and better,' she muttered, frown lines appearing between her brows. 'Valentine's Day blows.'

Damn. Cash would have to add blow alongside screwed as words Lucy should never utter around him.

'Couldn't agree more. Valentine's Day is overcommercialised crap for schmucks, but it's what we'll sign up for.'

'Just shoot me now,' she said, looking so woeful he couldn't help but smile.

'Don't all women dream of hearts and flowers and verbose declarations of love skywritten in fireworks until death us do part?'

She stiffened and squared her shoulders. 'Not this one.'

'Go on, admit it. You want a happily ever after as much as the next girl.' She had such an untouchable quality, he couldn't resist teasing her.

But he wasn't expecting to see genuine hurt in her expressive eyes. Hurt he didn't want to be responsible for.

'Hey, I was kidding...' He reached out to touch her hand and she snatched it away.

'Forget it.' She stood so abruptly the chair scraped loudly against the patio tiles. 'I'll start drawing up plans for the garden and get an itemised quote to you by the weekend.'

'Sure.' He should be rapt she'd agreed to his outlandish suggestion to pose as his girlfriend. So why the guilty niggle that he'd pushed her into doing something she'd rather not? 'We'll need to meet to go over our dating story, to strategise, stuff like that. How about dinner tomorrow?'

He deliberately chose a date-like rendezvous, to see if she lightened up enough to pull off this charade. Because the last thing he needed was for people to realise they weren't really a couple and he was doing this for the PR.

'Dinner?' She made it sound as if he'd invited her to leap into the Yarra River naked on a frigid winter's day.

'That's what *couples* do,' he said, his emphasis not lost when acceptance downturned her mouth.

'Yeah, you're right.' She visibly brightened. 'But I get to choose the place.'

Was it a power thing? Did Lucy need to feel in control and that was what her funk was about? Fine. Frankly, he didn't care where they ate as long as they put in a good show for the competition and he didn't lose his clients and his business.

'Not a problem. Text me the details.'

'Done.'

She waved and almost ran down the steps in her haste to escape. How they were going to pull off togetherness for the cameras he'd never know.

As he gathered papers and flipped his laptop shut she called out, 'Cash?'

He glanced up, surprised by the mischievous glint in her eyes. 'Yeah?'

'Tomorrow night? Hope you like it spicy.'

With a jaunty half-salute she was gone, leaving him confused by her hot and cold act and looking forward to tomorrow night more than was good for him.

That evening, Lucy picked up a half-garlic, half-ham-and-pineapple pizza on the way to supper with Gram. She hoped their favourite comfort food would do just that: provide comfort when she told Gram how she was obtaining the money to save her house.

Gram wouldn't be impressed. The last of the great romantics, Gram believed everyone deserved a lifetime of love. It had taken her six months after the initial separation to stop asking Lucy if there was any chance of reconciliation with Adrian; and the only reason she'd ceased badgering was because Lucy had finally told her the truth. That Adrian was a serial philanderer with a penchant for spending his considerable wealth buying the affection of women other than his wife.

Gram had never mentioned his name again, which suited Lucy just fine. For while the hurt had faded following the discovery of Adrian's indiscretions, the shame hadn't. She'd been seduced by his world, had fallen for the glitz and glamour his wealth provided as much as she'd fallen for him. The designer clothes, the flashy car, the whirlwind of parties. She'd loved it all.

Their marriage had seemed effortless, almost too good to be true. Which figured, considering that it was.

So it wasn't any great surprise she'd shut herself off from that world when it fell apart. She'd sold off her designer gear, ditched the fancy haircuts and make-up, and found solace in gardening.

She liked dirt trickling through her fingers. She liked the solitude. She liked the small of damp earth and freshly cut grass. There was an inherent honesty in being so close with nature, a comfort she hadn't found elsewhere.

Gram had understood, had fostered her love for the outdoors and Adrian soon became a distant memory. But Gram's romantic nature couldn't be suppressed and she occasionally probed for news of Lucy's dates, or 'possibilities' as Gram liked to call her infrequent forays into dinner or a movie.

The truth was, Lucy didn't socialise much. She dated occasionally, laid-back guys she'd met at the mulch supplier or tool shop. Blue-collar guys the exact opposite of Adrian.

But she hadn't felt a buzz in a long time…until today, when Cash had kissed her.

Not good.

She'd done her best to rationalise her reaction for the rest of the day, attributing the spark she'd felt as dormant hormones getting a kick-start.

While that might be true, it didn't explain the insane yearning to do it again. To see if it had been a fluke, a one-off. To see if he could make her whole body come alive for the first time in for ever.

Cursing under her breath, she let herself into Gram's cottage through the back door and dumped the pizza on the counter.

'Hope you're hungry, Gram,' she called out, dishing the pizza.

'Starving. Be there in a sec,' Gram called out from the bedroom.

Good. A few seconds gave Lucy time to mentally rehearse her spiel. Delivery was key if Gram was to accept her crazy scheme.

'All done.' Gram shuffled into the kitchen, drying her hands on a towel. 'No more surprises.'

Curious, Lucy placed their plates at the table and returned to the sink to fill two glasses with water. 'What were you up to?'

'Going through your grandfather's files. Making sure there were no more nasty debts ready to pop up and make our life hell.'

Lucy nodded, saddened by the secrets Pops must've kept from those he loved. 'Good idea.'

Gram sat at the table and licked her lips. 'Okay. This is your second visit in one day and you bring pizza. What's going on?'

Lucy slipped an arm around Gram's shoulders and squeezed. 'Never could fool you.'

Gram's eyes twinkled as Lucy took a seat. 'My girl, you forget that I was your age, once—and I tried every trick in the book.'

'I'm not sure you will have tried my latest trick, Gram.' Lucy toyed with the cheese oozing over the crust of her pizza. 'You know that plan I mentioned to secure the fifty grand? It's all set.'

Gram's mouth dropped open before it closed with an audible snap. 'I hoped...I mean, I thought you were dreaming...how—?'

'One of my clients wants a complete redesign of his garden. The quote is about fifty thousand.'

Gram's eyes widened in horror. 'I can't take that much of your hard-earned money off you. It wouldn't be right.'

Lucy should have known this wouldn't be easy. 'Gram, you raised me. I owe you everything and this is the least I can do to repay you.'

'Family don't need repaying.' Her lips set in a mutinous line. 'I won't take it.'

'So you'd rather move out? Live in a one-room rented bedsit somewhere?'

Gram glanced away but not before Lucy had glimpsed fear. 'If that's what it takes. Your grandfather caused this problem, not you, and I won't have you paying for his sins.'

Lucy admired Gram's pride. In fact, she empathised. She hadn't wanted anything to do with Adrian once she'd discovered his lies and pride had prevented her from taking the generous settlement he'd offered.

Pops had called her foolish at the time but Gram had been quick to silence him, telling him to mind his own business. No, she couldn't fault Gram for not wanting to take such a hefty sum of money. But it meant Lucy would have to embellish her offer to make it more appealing: namely, appeal to Gram's romantic side.

'That garden I'm doing? It's in exchange for accompanying the client to a few functions.'

Predictably, Gram perked up and lost her stubborn pout. 'What functions? And who's this client?'

'Cashel Burgess.'

A small dent appeared between Gram's brows. 'Why does his name sound familiar?'

'He's in the papers a fair bit.' Understatement, considering the number of times his handsome face graced the society pages. The way he put it, his socialising was purely work, but she wondered how many times he'd blurred the lines between personal and professional with his clients.

Not that it was any of her business, but the thought of his many dalliances made her stomach churn and she nudged away the plate of pizza.

'He's a financial advisor to the stars.'

Gram fixed her with a steely glare. 'Doesn't sound like your type.'

'He's not, but he's a nice enough guy, he asked for my help and I agreed.'

'On the proviso you get fifty thousand dollars for making over his garden.' Gram shook her head. 'What am I missing here? Sounds to me like the guy's desperate or crazy or both, offering to pay you to attend a few functions.'

Lucy should've known Gram wouldn't give up easily. The last thing she needed was Gram getting ideas about her fake relationship with Cash, but looked as if she'd have to tell her the rest.

'He's not desperate.' Lucy slid her electronic tablet out of her bag and plugged Cash's name into a search engine. 'Take a look at the guy.'

She flipped the screen towards Gram, who clutched at her heart. 'Oh my Lordy, the man's swoon-worthy.'

Lucy laughed. Not many men made Gram's swoon-worthy cut. Over the years, the limited list included Frank Sinatra, Rock Hudson, Elvis and more recently George Clooney. High praise indeed for her pretend boyfriend.

'He looks like that handsome young man in *The Notebook*.' Gram stared at her with renewed interest. 'Not every day my granddaughter gets to parade around with a Ryan Gosling lookalike.'

Lucy stared at the picture of Cash on the screen, tilting her head to one side, and had to admit Gram was right.

Ryan was excessively cute and they'd both cried buckets during that movie. Five times.

Great, now every time she had to look at Cash she'd be imagining Ryan and those sexy scenes…best not go there.

'You know, maybe this isn't such a bad idea after all.'

Gram's gaze strayed from the screen long enough for Lucy to see that familiar calculated, matchmaking gleam. 'Going out with a young man of that calibre can only be good.'

'This is a business arrangement, Gram, nothing more.'

Predictably, Gram ignored her warning tone and continued. 'I know there's a lot more to this than you're telling me, missie, but you've got a good heart and a smart head on your shoulders. I trust your judgement.'

'Does this mean you'll take the money?'

'We'll see,' Gram muttered, her brusqueness tempered by a warm smile, and Lucy took it as a win. 'Now, let's eat.'

Lucy was only too happy to comply, but as she bit into the gooey cheese she wondered how smart her judgement had been when she'd let Cash kiss her earlier that day.

And enjoyed it.

CHAPTER FOUR

LUCY DIDN'T LIKE feeling powerless. She'd felt it once before, around the time Adrian dumped a whole heap of whoop-ass on her head in the form of a divorce. She'd done everything humanly possible in the ensuing years to ensure she never felt that way again.

But following Cash's impulsive kiss yesterday morning, that was exactly how she'd felt. Powerless. Out of her depth.

He'd done it to rattle her probably. Or just because he could. Guys like him were used to kissing women every day of the week. A power play? An ego trip? Whatever the reason, she didn't want to bring it up again by asking him.

But she did have to reassert control and that meant putting him on the back foot this time.

She'd assumed meeting him for dinner in a pokey, no-frills Indian restaurant in the heart of Melbourne's busy CBD would do just that.

She'd been wrong.

From the moment he'd strutted into the place wearing faded denim and a navy polo top, she'd been fidgety and edgy and altogether too flustered.

The guy looked incredible.

She'd never seen him in anything other than slick suits.

She preferred him that way: hands-off. The kind of guy she'd never go for again.

But this new, improved version of Cash, his fingers stained orange from eating chicken tikka with his hands, sweat beading his brow from the fiery prawn vindaloo and the constant appreciative moans after every mouthful?

Way too appealing. And ruining her plans to rattle him good and proper.

'How did you find this place?' He dipped a piece of naan bread into a golden dahl before popping it into his mouth, his rapturous expression making her increasingly uncomfortable.

Could he look any more...*orgasmic*? Damn.

'Stumbled on it a lifetime ago, been coming here ever since,' she said, ladling more lamb korma on her plate in an effort to keep her hands busy and her mind firmly on the meal. 'The quality of the food more than makes up for the lack in décor.'

'I don't give a flying fig how a place looks if the food tastes this good.' He scooped up a healthy serve of aloo gobi and spooned it into his mouth to prove it.

'Aren't you just full of surprises?' she said under her breath, not sure whether to laugh or cry at this turn of events.

Pretending to be Cash's girlfriend would've been easier when she didn't like the guy. Seeing this relaxed, easy to conform side of him? Not good for her peace of mind.

She didn't want to like him.

Not with the memory of that kiss on constant replay in her head.

'Go on, admit it.' He swiped at his mouth with a serviette. 'You've misjudged me.'

Great. Not only was the guy easy-going and gorgeous, he was astute too.

'Don't know what you're talking about.' She crossed her fingers under the table for telling the little white lie.

'Yeah, you do,' he said, impossibly smug as he leaned back in his chair and studied her with an intensity that burned hotter than the curries she'd eaten. 'Because of all that beat-up crap in the media, you thought I'm used to dining in five-star restaurants and I'd hate a place like this.'

Lucy added intelligent to his growing list of attributes. Double damn.

She chose her response carefully, not wanting to give away too much. 'Not an entirely ludicrous assumption, considering you're in the papers every week attending some fancy shindig with a famous woman on your arm.'

'You've kept tabs on me?' His conceited grin infuriated her. 'Why, Lucy, I didn't know you cared.'

'I don't,' she snapped, instantly regretting her terse answer when his grin widened. 'It's called Googling and being prepared, considering I'll be your girlfriend for the next week.'

'So you plugged me into a search engine to check me out. Even better.' He winked. 'Discover anything interesting?'

'Only that you have too much time on your hands by the number of flashy functions you attend.'

And that he had a thing for vacuous blondes. She decided to keep that particular insight to herself.

'Networking is a huge part of my job,' he said, his grin fading as he reached for a water. 'I get most of my clients by word of mouth.'

'So why should the ramblings of one woman threaten to derail a reputation you've built over the years?'

His eyes widened in appreciation. 'You have done your homework.'

He gulped the water and set the glass on the table. 'Unfortunately, the referral network my business thrives on is pretty fragile. Stars in the TV industry can be fickle and gossip is easily spread. All it takes is one false rumour and…'

He shook his head. 'I won't let that happen. I've worked too damn hard to build up my business to let it be ruined by a vindictive woman.'

His honesty impressed her. 'So what happened to make this woman so intent on revenge? Did you break her heart?'

'Didn't get that close.' He screwed up his face in disgust. 'She wanted more than one date, I didn't, and she didn't take the knock-back kindly. Next thing I know she's threatening all sorts of bizarre scenarios. I got the impression she's desperate for publicity for her fledgling career and others I've spoken to aren't impressed by her antics off screen in general.'

'That's sad.'

'Don't feel sorry for her. I'm the one she can ruin with her craziness.'

Lucy leaned forward and patted his hand. 'Don't worry, I'll be the epitome of a sane girlfriend to counteract your loony ex.'

'She's not my ex—'

'Kidding.' Lucy tried to move her hand away but not fast enough, as Cash turned his over and captured hers.

'It's kinda nice having you want to protect me.' His thumb brushed her pulse point and she almost leaped off her chair. 'Something tells me we're going to be very good together.'

For one insane moment, with Cash holding her hand

and staring at her with blatant interest, she could almost believe him.

'And something tells me if we don't get our stories straight your reputation isn't the only one about to flush down the toilet.' She withdrew her hand. It did little for the residual tingle in her palm. 'So what's the spin we put on our faux romance?'

'We stick to the truth as much as possible,' he said, looking way too comfortable for a guy about to perpetuate a big, fat lie, while she all but squirmed at the thought of being filmed for some hokey Valentine's Day fundraiser. 'We met six months ago through a mutual friend but haven't started dating 'til recently.'

'And the fact you've kept me hidden away while parading around town with your usual arm candy?'

'You sound jealous.' He smirked.

'I'd have to care first,' she said, shooting him a sickly sweet smile.

'I'm a man who likes to keep his personal and professional lives separate, so that's why we haven't gone public yet. Those other women? Business.'

'More like monkey business,' she muttered, earning another wink for her trouble. 'Tell me more about these functions we have to attend.'

'We're being briefed tomorrow apparently. All I know is we attend a picnic, an eighties-inspired disco and a roller-skating event, before the ball on Valentine's Day.'

Lucy pretended to stick two fingers down her throat and gag.

He grimaced. 'Yeah, sounds like a pain in the ass.'

'The things we do for love, huh?' She batted her eyelashes and he laughed, the lines crinkling the corners of his eyes adding depth to his face.

'Want to know what I think?' He leaned forward.

'Do I have a choice?'

'Keep doing that.' He jabbed a finger in her direction. 'If we can keep doing this trading quips thing when the cameras are around, they'll think we're a real couple for sure.'

'True,' she said, remembering the many times Gram and Pops would bicker over the smallest thing. Other couples she'd seen over the years too. That should've been her first indication something was wrong with her marriage: the fact that Adrian was far too civilised and they never fought. No relationship was that perfect. She knew that now.

'Did I pass?'

She blinked away memories better left suppressed. 'What?'

'Did I pass your test, the one you set by inviting me to dinner here?'

'Test?' she asked, looking as incredulous as possible.

'Come on, Lucy. I knew from the minute you invited me here that you had something up your sleeve. You couldn't wait to get me out of my comfort zone.'

She nodded begrudgingly. 'I like a guy who can adjust to his surroundings. Especially a stuck-up, wealthy guy, who I assumed wouldn't know dahl from a dollar.'

'Careful. I could've sworn you said you like me.' He ignored her veiled insults and focused on the one thing she wished he wouldn't. 'Which is kinda nice, considering I really like you.'

He was teasing, she knew that, but the small part of her that had been starved of male attention for too long lapped it up.

'Good to see you practising for the cameras,' she said, hoping to defuse some of the tension gripping her by gulping her mango lassi.

Sadly, the cool fruity yoghurt did little for the heat racing through her body and making her yearn for things she shouldn't. Like Cash. Naked.

'Why do you do that?' His hand snaked across the table to touch her wrist. 'Pretend like there's no way in hell I could find you remotely attractive.'

'Because I know your type and I'm not it.' She barked out a bitter laugh and gestured at her faded skinny jeans and thigh-length red cotton T. 'Look at me. I wear khaki work shorts and singlets or denim and cotton.' She pointed to her face. 'No make-up.' She tugged on the ends of her cropped hair. 'Without a foil or high-light in sight.'

His expression morphed from playful to sincere. 'Did you stop to think that maybe that's why I like you? That I don't go for all that artifice when it matters? That appearances can be deceptive and I prefer to judge a person on what's inside?'

She could've applauded his valiant speech if not for one thing: if what she'd researched was true, he'd spent his entire life proving the opposite of everything he'd just said.

'Let's stick to the programme, okay?' She signalled for the bill. 'We both know this thing between us is fake. No need to label it as anything else.'

Cash frowned, and looked set to belabour the point, but thankfully the waiter's speedy arrival took care of that.

Good. The last thing Lucy needed was Cash trying to convince her that he was deeper than her perception. A perception fast being challenged by this surprisingly sweet, sexy man.

CHAPTER FIVE

THE NEXT MORNING, Lucy met with the last person on the planet she'd want to spend time with.

A stylist.

She liked the way she looked. She liked wearing comfortable, versatile clothes. She liked maintaining a no-fuss haircut, even if she did look as if she'd just got out of bed and headed to work most days.

But she liked the thought of saving Gram's house more, and desperate times called for affirmative action: like updating her wardrobe, her hairstyle and her look.

Not that she was doing this to impress Cash. She'd taken pride in her appearance once, had loved the expensive fashions she'd worn during her marriage, had adored her artistic hairdresser, had spent an inordinate amount on make-up.

But no matter how prettied up she'd been, Adrian had cheated on her anyway and she'd shut away her inner fashion guru a long time ago.

However, being filmed as part of Cash's fundraiser changed the playing field. And after his impassioned speech last night about not judging on appearances, she felt guilty.

Just because she didn't go in for frippery any more didn't mean he could neglect his public image, and she'd be doing him a disservice by rocking up to his fancy functions in ripped denim and pilled cotton.

He'd been nothing but lovely last night and her subtle antagonism seemed to make him laugh all the harder.

She had no intention of falling for his charm, which he was obviously used to laying on thick with the girls, but somewhere between the potato bondas and the Madras chicken curry she'd grown to respect him a tad.

And she was starting to regret having done the one thing he said he didn't do: judge on appearances.

Because she had. Judged him. By the house he lived in, by the clothes he wore, by the company he kept.

Despite her preconceptions, the Cash she'd enjoyed a delicious Indian meal with in that tatty diner? Unpretentious, easy-going and able to laugh at himself.

She'd made a snap decision on leaving the restaurant: if she had to spend a week in his company, the least she could do was lighten up.

Not every guy was the enemy and, sadly, the years of self-imposed singledom had turned her into a cynic.

So that was why she was here, in one of Melbourne's iconic department stores, consulting with an elegant woman who had nothing on her mind but making Lucy spend as much money as humanly possible.

'You have a good eye for fashion.' The fifty-something woman with a blonde coif, wearing a tight black shift and towering stiletto pumps, stood back and appraised her with blatant shock. 'Every piece you've chosen looks like it has been made for you.'

'I like clothes,' Lucy said, her simple statement earning a beaming smile from FashionZilla.

'I'll be right back with the perfect sandals to go with that sheath.' The consultant bustled away, leaving Lucy standing in a small room that looked like something out of *Arabian Nights*.

She spun around, feeling like Carrie in *Sex and the City*, glamorous and chic, the simple strapless red sheath reflected back to her tenfold in the surrounding floor-length mirrors.

Her hands skimmed the shot silk, savouring the slide of expensive fabric. Out of all the outfits she'd tried on, this had made her heart flutter the most.

She remembered this heady feeling: of choosing the perfect outfit, confident she looked good in it. All the clothes she'd worn back then had been about her: making her feel good. Sure, she'd appreciated Adrian's compliments, but after a frugal upbringing it had been like a kid let loose in a candy shop and she'd revelled in it.

Which was the exact reason why she'd left it all behind.

She hadn't wanted to be reminded of her foolishness. Had she been so wrapped up in the frivolity of her indulgent lifestyle that she'd been oblivious to her husband's indiscretions? Or worse, had she used her privileged life as a deliberate distraction from the warning signs?

She hadn't thought so at the time, or during the many months after she'd dissected the disastrous fallout, but on the odd occasion when she allowed her mind to drift she wondered if she'd been blinded to the truth by the glitz she'd grown to love.

The consultant hurried back into the room and thrust a pair of sparkly stilettos at her. 'Here, try these.'

Lucy had a distinct Dorothy from *The Wizard of Oz* moment as she slipped on the sparkly crimson heels. If only she could click her heels and vanish back to the staid normality of her life before she'd discovered the truth about Pops, the threat to Gram's house and the craziness of agreeing to pose as Cash's girlfriend.

'What do you think?' The consultant fussed around her, smoothing non-existent creases and adjusting the zip. 'You'll make quite the impression in this outfit whatever the occasion.'

The occasion would be the Valentine's Day ball and a most welcome conclusion to her week-long zaniness posing as Cash's girlfriend.

Once her obligations were done, she could throw herself wholeheartedly into his landscaping job.

But as she stared at her startling image in the mirror, she had a thought. How would she interact with Cash after this week was done? Would they revert to their previous cool relationship or would the week of forced proximity and faked romance change things?

Ideally, she'd go back to ignoring his overtures and he'd go back to making millions. In reality, Lucy knew a week of spending time together, sparring and joking, would blur the boundaries.

'Shall I start packaging your choices?' The stylist picked up her clipboard and started ticking items off her list. 'Just to clarify: you're taking the jade waffle-knit jacket, the aubergine skirt suit, the black pencil skirt, the tribal print dress, the quilted puffer jacket, the floral flip skirt, and the formal sheath you're wearing.'

This was the time for Lucy's sanity to return. She should bolt from the store while she had the chance. Instead, she found herself reluctantly nodding. 'Yes, thanks.'

The woman's eyes glittered at what would be healthy commission. 'And the shoes to complement the outfits? Black patent leather kitten heels, the knee-high boots and the crimson evening stilettos?'

'Those too,' Lucy said, her resigned sigh earning an odd look from the stylist.

'You get changed while I start putting these purchases through.' The stylist wiggled a card out from a stash on a nearby table. 'And if you're interested, our in-store hairstylist is offering seventy-five per cent off all services to customers who spend over five hundred dollars here.'

Considering Lucy had just spent double that on replenishing her wardrobe, she definitely qualified. Lucy thanked her, took the card and slipped back into the dressing room to change back into her jeans and 'I HEART DIRT' T-shirt.

She'd come this far in her lunacy. Why not go the whole hog and get her hair done too?

Feeling chirpier than she had in ages, she hummed the latest pop song under her breath as she changed, surprisingly eager to see Cash's expression when she met him at the PR firm's head office to launch the fundraiser later today.

Cash wished Lucy had agreed to him picking her up. He'd wanted to make a statement by the two of them walking into the plush offices of GR8 4U Public Relations together, showing the rest of the competition that they were a couple and loving it.

What a joke.

About the only thing Lucy loved was roasting him over hot coals.

He'd hoped she'd thaw towards him over dinner last night. And he'd been making inroads too. Until their conversation had drifted towards appearances and Lucy had frozen him out faster than a naked explorer in Antarctica.

Lucy had a confidence problem. Made sense she hid behind a tough exterior, flinging out barbs at random to hold him off.

Was it him or all guys? Had some guy done a number on her?

And that was when it hit him. He hadn't even asked if she had a guy in her life. He'd assumed not, considering she'd agreed to his crazy scheme. But what if there was a boyfriend in the picture and that was why she didn't like him? Because she needed to maintain distance between them?

Would certainly explain her frosty behaviour. Maybe she needed the money so badly she'd agreed to it, but had to explain it to her bloke who'd stipulated cool and hands-off?

Little wonder she'd freaked out over that kiss.

Damn, he'd played this all wrong.

However, considering he now stood in a glass-panelled conference room awaiting the arrival of his girlfriend to kick-start proceedings, it was too late to change tack now.

Barton accepted champagne from a passing waiter and sidled up to him. 'Your girl going to show?'

''Course,' Cash said, wishing he sounded more confident. 'She'll be here.'

Barton leaned closer. 'So what did you offer her to partake in this charade?'

Cash knew he could trust Bart but this wasn't the best place to be discussing his fake relationship. He lowered his voice. 'She's landscaping my garden for a hefty price.'

Respect gleamed in Bart's eyes. 'A savvy businesswoman. Good for her.'

'Yeah, Lucy's definitely full of surprises,' he said, a

second before he caught sight of a sexy brunette hovering in the doorway.

She wore a tailored linen suit the colour of ripe plums, the knee-length skirt halfway between demure and downright naughty, with a hint of black lacy camisole at her cleavage. Her bare legs shimmered bronze, highlighted by a pair of sky-high patent leather pumps.

When he tore his gaze away from those sensational legs, he noticed her hair, cut in a stylish shaggy bob, caramel highlights adding a sheen to the sleek brown waves.

That was when he finally looked at the woman's eyes. And almost keeled over.

Large brown eyes the colour of his favourite coffee beans, ringed by subtle kohl, fringed in long lashes designed to flirt.

Eyes that had pinned him with unswerving censure last night.

Eyes that he'd let himself drown in given half a chance.

Lucy.

'Yowza,' Bart said, his glass paused halfway to his mouth. 'Is that your girl?'

When Cash unglued his tongue from the roof of his mouth a few moments later, he managed a mumbled, 'Yeah,' for his friend before making a beeline for the door.

The closer he got, he noticed something else about Lucy that shocked him.

She wasn't looking at him with reservation or caution. Uh-uh. As he strode towards her she stared at him with defiance, as if daring him to say something about the new her and make a mess of this.

Not bloody likely.

For all he knew, this could be a test, to see if he liked

her more in the new clothes and with a new haircut, considering he'd said the opposite last night.

So he did the only thing possible. The one thing guaranteed to keep from putting his foot in his mouth.

He kissed her.

CHAPTER SIX

THE FIRST THING that registered with Cash was the peppermint-infused lip-gloss Lucy wore and how delicious she tasted.

The second? Muted applause and laughter.

Lucy gave him a little shove and he broke the kiss, dazed to find a roomful of people looking on. Some wore goofy grins, some—the competition, he assumed—sized him up, and some—guys mostly—looked jealous.

Another glance at Lucy and he couldn't blame them. His kiss had made her blush, and her rosy cheeks added to the sparkle in her eyes.

She looked radiant. Luminous. Like a woman crazy about her man.

Wow, who knew she could act so well?

'By that greeting, I assume you approve of my grand entrance?' she said, low enough so only he could hear.

'It's normal for a guy to greet his girlfriend with a kiss. Get used to it.'

He hated how abrupt he sounded but she'd seriously thrown him with her perfect girlfriend act. It was what he wanted, what he needed to stave off disaster for his business, so why did this new Lucy disarm him so much?

Hurt flickered in her eyes and he silently cursed.

'Sorry. Guess I'm nervous,' he said, taking hold of her

hand, not surprised when she stalled momentarily before falling into step beside him. 'We've got a few minutes before the launch starts. Let's go find a quiet place to chat.'

She nodded, her hand relaxing in his the closer they got to a secluded corner of the room, behind a semi-opaque glass screen.

They'd barely reached the corner when he blurted, 'Do you have a boyfriend?'

'No.' Her eyes widened, those mascaraed lashes adding to the vamp-versus-virgin thing she had going on. 'Do you seriously think I would've agreed to your dumbass scheme if I did?'

Relief overcame his uncharacteristic nerves at her typical blunt response. 'Maybe you both needed the money?'

'And maybe you need a lobotomy.' She stepped closer, so close he felt her breath brush his ear, so close he could smell her subtle perfume, an intoxicating blend of flowers and spice. 'Yeah, I'm doing it for the money. Why I need it? None of your damn business. So quit acting like an idiot and start behaving like a solicitous boyfriend.'

Suitably chastised, and feeling like a bit of a heel for kissing her first and asking the boyfriend question later, he flashed her a smile he hoped would placate. 'I thought I was, with that kiss.'

She blushed again, prompting him to wonder if she reddened during other activities involving kissing.

Her nose crinkled adorably. 'That kiss was all show, just like you.'

There she went again, implying he was shallow. So he retaliated in kind. 'Hey, I'm not the one strutting in here trying to make a big impression.'

The moment the words slipped out, he wished he could take them back. She crumpled a little. Nothing overt, but a slight slump to her shoulders, a dejected quirk to her glossed lips.

Bugger.

She snatched her hand out of his and he let her, feeling like the bastard he was. 'Look, I'm sorry, that was way out of line.'

Her lips compressed, as if she didn't want to say something she'd regret. Pity he hadn't done the same thing a moment ago.

'I know this is a weak excuse, but I'm not very good at handling surprises.' He never had been. Since his mum abandoned him when he was four and his dad morphed into a cold, demanding man who saw nothing in him but reminders of the woman he'd rather forget, Cash had learnt to appreciate stability.

Surprises sucked.

He touched her arm, wishing he could convey how sorry he was for acting like an ass when all she'd done was try to be the model girlfriend he needed to make this stupid scheme work. 'Guess you threw me, strutting in here like a sex goddess.'

Her startled gaze flew to his.

'What? You don't know that every guy in the room wants to take you on the boardroom table?'

This time, her mouth dropped open too.

He swore and stuck a finger between his tie and shirt collar, trying to loosen it so he could get some air to his lungs and ultimately his brain. 'Damn it, what the hell's wrong with me?'

'Where do you want me to start?' she said, the corners of her mouth easing into a semi-smile. 'But for what it's worth, I appreciate honesty.'

'So you think it's a good thing every guy in here wants to—'

'You're exaggerating,' she said, her coy smile going some way to soothing the monumental stuff-up he'd made of the last few minutes.

For a guy who prided himself on knowing what to say and when with his clients, he'd really made a fool of himself.

'What I was referring to when I said I appreciated honesty was you admitting that you don't like surprises. They do seem to make you act a little nuts.'

'A little?' His sarcasm drew another smile. 'Trust me, I'm not usually such a putz.'

'So it's not you, it's me?'

She was teasing. A good thing, considering the disastrous faux pas he'd made in blurting his innermost thoughts. *He* hadn't been lying when he'd said he wanted to take her on the boardroom table, but why the hell did he have to reveal it like that? In fact, what was he thinking revealing it at all?

'It's not how incredible you look, because you do. And it's not the shock of seeing you dolled up, because you already know I think you're beautiful without all the fancy outer trappings. It's...'

Cash trailed off, unable to articulate the truth.

Because what made him go a bit crazy wasn't any of that stuff he'd just said, but the fact when he'd caught sight of Lucy he'd forgotten the real reason they were here—to pretend they had a relationship for the sake of their respective businesses—and wanted her for real.

As far as curve balls went, it was huge. This charade had barely kicked off and he already wanted her in a way that went beyond their deal.

It confused the hell out of him. Cash didn't get involved with women for a reason. He understood business. He understood the comfort and certainty of money. He understood how getting close to a woman could foster dependency and love, only to have the lot ripped away, leaving pain and devastation in its wake.

Every time he visited his dad, Ronnie, he saw the evidence firsthand. And it gutted him. His dad might not have been the easiest man to live with when he'd been younger, but he was the only parent Cash had ever known. To see a man cut down in his prime like that all because of a woman? No way would Cash ever open himself up for that kind of desolation.

'You okay?' Lucy was staring at him quizzically.

'Not really.' He glanced at her, those beautiful brown eyes, way too trusting and filled with concern, and shook his head. 'But it's my problem, not yours. Let's just concentrate on getting through this week without either of us going loco, okay?'

'Sounds like a plan,' she said, slipping her hand through his elbow when he offered it.

Now all Cash needed was for his head to get with the plan. A clear-cut, no-nonsense, business arrangement between two people who barely knew each other.

Something he'd need to remind himself constantly if Lucy rocked up to any more functions intent on *surprising* him.

Sex goddess.

Those two little words echoed through Lucy's head: relentless, taunting, flattering.

She'd wanted to make an impression on Cash, not send the poor guy bonkers. Because that was what had happened the moment she'd tottered in here, out of practice in high heels. He'd been acting like a crazy person. Complimentary one second, snappy the next.

Then he had to go and blurt that crap again, about

liking her for who she was, sans fancy clothes, make-up and new haircut, and she was back to square one: liking him more than was good for her.

She could attribute his bamboozlement to excellent acting skills: a guy trying to woo her in the hope of making their interaction look more real for the cameras.

Except for one factor: he'd appeared seriously rattled when he'd admitted that he didn't like surprises. In fact, he looked like a guy who'd had a few nasty shocks in his lifetime. And she was in trouble, because that hint of vulnerability beneath his suave exterior? Made him all the more appealing.

'How are you holding up?' he murmured in her ear, sending a shiver of illicit longing through her.

She could blame her physical reaction to Cash on the fact she hadn't had a date in a while—like six months—but she knew better. Cash was the whole package: handsome, dry sense of humour and, she'd finally accepted, downright nice.

'I'm fine,' she said, wishing the organisers would wind up their explanatory spiel so she could get out of here.

She was looking forward to getting out of these clothes and finding solace in gardening. When Lucy was feeling unsettled, she liked nothing better than to vent her frustration by digging and hoeing and slashing. How unsettled she was feeling right now? She'd need to spend the rest of the day with her hands in the dirt.

Just thinking about it had her mentally listing her planting to-do list for early February: okra, kohlrabi, radish, parsnip, leeks, collards. She'd head home as soon as this shindig was over and go berserk in the veggie patch. Perfect way to work off the edginess.

'You don't look okay.' He squeezed her hand, which he had to hold for appearances' sake, apparently. 'You look like a girl in need of a double-shot latte or a family-size block of chocolate.'

He paused, shot her a sideways glance she had no hope of interpreting. 'I can provide both at my place if you need to unwind, debrief, whatever, after this.'

Lucy was tempted. Really tempted. The thought of getting to know her enigmatic *boyfriend* better appealed.

But after their bizarre exchange earlier and the tension-fraught last hour, listening to the organisers drone on about functions they'd have to attend, rules and regulations, and instructions to ham up the romance for the cameras, she was exhausted.

She needed to cut her losses and run, before her physically and mentally drained self did something silly: such as decide she wanted more than caffeine as comfort and hurl herself into Cash's arms.

'Thanks for the offer, but I'm heading home.'

'Okay.' His disappointment mirrored hers but she steeled her resolve. Shrugging off the feeling, she silently repeated to herself what seemed to be becoming her new mantra:

Must. Not. Fall. For. Fake. Boyfriend.

Lucy had almost reached her car when the sound of footsteps pounding the pavement behind her made her turn around.

Great, the one man she'd been all too eager to escape was running after her as if he had demons on his tail.

As if Cash hadn't unnerved her enough over the last hour or two. She needed to make a quick getaway before she took him up on that offer of a mega block of chocolate. Because she knew she wasn't far from doing something stupid, like succumbing to the temptation of a soft, leather couch and a cosy evening with a guy who made her pulse race.

'Did I forget something?' She congratulated herself on injecting the right amount of cool into her voice, when in fact his proximity made everything, from her knees to her resolve, wobble.

'No, but I did.' He skidded to a stop in front of her. 'I wanted to give you this.'

He whipped a cellophane-wrapped, long-stemmed red rose from behind his back and held it out to her. 'A token for your forgiveness?'

Confused, she accepted the rose and held it up to her nose, inhaling the sweet, rich fragrance. 'Unless you stuffed up after I left, there's nothing to forgive.'

'Yeah, there is.' He dragged a hand through his hair, while the other tugged at the knot of his tie. Interesting. Cash looked as edgy as she felt. 'I made a mess of things today.'

She shook her head. 'We cleared all that up—'

'Let me finish.' He held up his hand and took a step closer. So close she could see the fine stubble already dotting his jaw. 'When I first saw you walk into that room, you blew me away. And I should've said so. I should've said you were the most beautiful woman in the room. That you looked sensational in that suit and your new haircut looks lovely and make-up merely accentuates your eyes and lips, which are gorgeous enough as it is.'

He puffed out a long breath. 'But I didn't say any of those things. I acted like a jerk because you threw me. And then you were exceptionally nice about the whole thing and...ah, hell, I'm doing it again. Rambling...'

Touched by the effect she seemed to have on this man, she patted his cheek with the rose. 'Thanks.'

'For being a jerk?'

'For taking the time to come after me and apologise, even though you didn't need to.' She stood on tiptoe and quickly kissed his cheek. 'I really appreciate the compliments.'

He must've caught something in her wistful tone, because he slid an arm around her waist and hauled her close.

'Want to know why I made an ass of myself?'

Struggling to deal with his proximity and battling the urge to wrap her arms around his waist, she nodded. 'You said you don't like surprises?'

'That too.' He glanced away but didn't release her. 'When I first saw you, all I could think was how much I wanted you. For real.'

'Oh.'

A pretty inadequate syllable, considering the riotous emotions cartwheeling through her.

'I know we're pretending for the next week, but want to hear something crazy?'

'I think you're going to tell me regardless,' she said, her dry response drawing a huge grin.

'Okay, here goes,' he said, resting his other hand on her hip, an intimate gesture that almost had her swooning against him. 'Don't be surprised if some time over the next week, I blur the lines between fantasy and reality.'

Lucy could've attributed all this to more of Cash's signature schmoozing. A guy used to attracting women. A guy seeing her as a challenge. A guy assuming their proximity over the next week would naturally lead to intimacy.

Except for one thing.

The genuine sincerity in his eyes and the complete lack of guile.

Cash wasn't doing a number on her.

He was being upfront and telling her exactly how he felt. Considering his confusion matched hers, she should be thankful for his honesty.

Instead, it only served to increase her trepidation.

She didn't need to feel empathy for Cash.

She needed to keep reminding herself that getting up close and personal with her fake boyfriend could only end badly. Especially when she'd be spending a month or two after this ended at his house, remodelling his garden.

With a soft sigh of regret, she slipped from his arms. 'Blurred lines will only complicate things.'

'True, but it might be kinda fun?'

Lucy almost capitulated right there and then, his cute, little-boy expression making her heart melt.

But she couldn't shirk her intrinsic insecurities so easily.

Was Cash only coming after her because of how she looked? Had her makeover impressed him that much that he now saw her as yet another attractive adjunct in his pretty world?

Deep down, she didn't think so. But she'd developed a hefty amount of self-preservation over the years and she couldn't let some articulate, intelligent guy who said all the right things and who happened to be drop-dead-gorgeous sway her.

'Thanks for the rose.' She unlocked her car before he said anything else to undermine her resolve.

'You're welcome.' He hesitated, as if about to say something else, before shaking his head almost imperceptibly. 'Enjoy the rest of your evening.'

'You too.'

Lucy fumbled the keys twice before inserting them

and starting the car. Yeah, her steely resolve to keep Cash at arm's length was working a treat. Not.

He waved as she drove away, struggling not to watch the lone figure in her rear-vision mirror, and resisting the insane impulse to turn around.

CHAPTER SEVEN

Lucy hovered in the doorway of Melbourne's premier hotel's function room, wishing she'd taken Cash up on his offer of a lift.

She hadn't socialised in a long while and rocking up to this kitschy eighties disco had the potential to unnerve her.

She'd told Cash she'd meet him here but one glance into the crowded room and she knew she'd made a mistake.

Everyone was paired off. Most were fellow competition couples but the dance floor was packed with other bodies, writhing and flinging their arms around and swaying to the beat.

Like her, they were dressed in eighties gear. Ludicrous. But the longer she stood there, watching a few Boy George and Prince wannabes doing their own version of a dance-off, the more she started to relax.

She loved eighties music and often played it on full blast while gardening.

Her favourites were Wham, Tears for Fears and Blondie, and she'd lost track of the number of times Gram had asked her to turn her iPod down when she'd been a kid.

She might have been born at the tail end of the eighties but the music seemed to have seeped into her regardless.

'Well, well, well. If it isn't Madonna.' Cash's warm breath fanned her ear and a surprising shiver of longing made her rub her bare arms.

She turned slowly, willing her stupid heart to stop racing. Her costume had seemed okay at home, but with Cash standing close behind her the midriff-baring lace top, denim mini and fishnet stockings made her feel naked.

Then she caught sight of him and some of her nerves eased. She laughed.

'Hey, I'm not supposed to be funny.' His hand slicked against his greased hair. 'I'm cool.'

'John Travolta was cool in *Grease*. You, on the other hand...' She stared at the skin-tight black leather pants moulding his legs to perfection, and the torso-hugging black T-shirt delineating every tempting ripple, and decided Cash was hot.

'What about me?' He squared his shoulders and darn if the action didn't accentuate his broad chest.

'You're late,' she said, her brusqueness not fooling him for a second, considering she had a hard time dragging her gaze away from his chest to focus on his face.

'Only five minutes.' He gestured at his outfit. 'It takes a while to look this good.'

'You're also out by a few years. Wasn't *Grease* released late seventies?'

''Seventy-eight to be precise but this kind of outfit?' He gestured towards the leather pants. 'Deserved an outing.'

She rolled her eyes and struggled not to laugh. 'Come on, the cameras will start filming in ten minutes.'

He grimaced. 'Don't remind me.'

She couldn't agree more. 'We don't have to win the

thing, remember? Let's have a few dances then get the hell out of here.'

'Agreed.' He placed a hand in the small of her back, sending a ripple of heat through her. 'Want a drink?'

Lucy didn't drink much alcohol and the last thing she needed was to have a drink go straight to her head.

'No thanks.'

'Then I guess we dance?'

He didn't give her time to agree, snagging her hand and tugging her towards the dance floor. While Lucy would never admit it to anyone, she liked the handholding. In fact, she liked being part of a couple, even a fake one.

Adrian might have been a selfish a-hole but in the early days, when she was blissfully unaware of his philandering? She'd loved the togetherness. Being part of a couple had made her feel secure in a way she'd never experienced.

While Gram and Pops had showered her with love and doted on her, she wondered if being an only child and without parents had inadvertently taken its toll. Maybe that had been the reason she'd lost her mind over her first steady boyfriend, married him and divorced him all within two years?

She'd examined that excuse at length when she'd first split from Adrian and summarily dismissed it. Because she knew why she'd married Adrian so quickly. She'd loved him. Had been head over heels. And she missed the closeness they'd once had more than anything.

She missed the banter of being with a guy. Missed the teasing and the laughter and the quick-firing barbs.

Cash was an expert at it and she knew that was what made her like him more than was good for her. Along with his sense of humour. His dedication to his business. His body…

That body.

She snuck a sideways glance, the coloured light reflected from a spinning silver disco ball smattering his skin like a kaleidoscope. It didn't detract from his distinguished features. In fact, as they edged onto the dance floor and a flash of gold highlighted the breadth of his shoulders, he looked like a god.

Then he stepped in close, slid an arm around her waist, hauled her against his body, and she was a goner.

The guy could *move*.

As Robbie Nevil belted out his hit song *C'est La Vie* Cash moulded his body to hers and danced as if he'd been born to do it.

She had no option but to loop her arms around his neck and go with it. Matching him step for step. Their bodies swaying and dipping. Creating a delicious friction that had every nerve ending in her body on high alert.

When one of his hands slid lower to cup her butt, she almost groaned. And when he applied pressure, bringing her pelvis in contact with his to show exactly how the heat they were creating affected him, she strained towards him.

That was when things got really interesting.

Dirty Dancing might have launched in the eighties but the version Lucy and Cash were producing was definitely an Oscar-winning sequel.

She writhed against him, shameless and wanton and hot. So hot.

The desire between them was palpable. Her skin burned with it. As the music blared and the bass beat pounded through her body Lucy gave herself over to the heady sensation of having vertical sex with her clothes on.

Because that was what they were doing.

Raunchy, debased, bold moves that made her cling to him or fall down in a puddle of lust at his feet.

She buzzed with the need to get naked, such a foreign feeling she almost stopped. But with her body plastered against Cash's and the insistent throb pounding through her, she couldn't have stopped if she'd wanted to.

Lucy had no idea when one song ended and the next began, because she'd never been so attuned to another human being before.

All she knew was this man, this moment.

It didn't surprise her when he nuzzled her neck, his lips grazing the tender skin beneath her ear, moving excruciatingly slowly towards her mouth.

Her head fell back and he claimed her lips in a sizzling kiss that sent her head spinning.

Her mouth opened as Cash applied the slightest pressure, and he didn't need a second invitation.

They exchanged hot, open-mouthed kisses for an eternity. Savage. Desperate. Unrestrained.

Lucy lost sense of time and place. All she knew was the incredible burning from the inside out, as if the whole dance floor were on fire.

The sound of raucous applause eventually filtered through her befuddled head as she realised the MC for the night had taken to the microphone and they hadn't noticed.

Cash wrenched his mouth from hers as they stared at each other in stunned silence, their chests heaving, breathing ragged.

The crowd eventually went back to looking at the stage and paying attention to the MC, but Lucy couldn't tear her gaze away from Cash's.

He didn't look like a guy who was acting.

He looked as smitten as she was.

Crap.

'You'd do anything for the cameras,' she said, eager to break the unbearable tension between them.

He ducked his head to whisper in her ear, 'If that was you play-acting, sweetheart, I'll double your landscaping fee.'

Her heart flipped at his call out. 'Then you owe me a hundred grand.'

He chuckled. 'Liar.'

She tossed her head, the scarf she'd tied under her hair flicking her cheek. 'Okay. So we kissed. Big deal. Bound to happen considering the music and the darkness and—'

'We're attracted to each other.' He ran a fingertip down her cheek. 'It's not a crime to admit it.'

Lucy gritted her teeth. No way could she admit to wanting Cash because that would be a giant complication waiting to happen.

She needed that fifty grand for Gram, not to get involved in some weird half-assed relationship that started out fake, yet involved very real sex.

Sex? Yikes. Was that where this was heading? She really was in trouble.

'Let's just keep our minds on the end goal, okay?'

'And what may that be?' His hand rested on her hip, an intimate gesture that tempted her to resume where they'd left off: but away from here with fewer clothes on. 'Seeing how far we can take this attraction?'

She sighed. 'Positive PR for you. Fifty thousand big ones for me.'

A shadow darkened his eyes and he removed his hand. 'So that's all this is to you? Easy money?'

'There's nothing easy about posing as your girlfriend for a week, big guy,' she said, aiming for levity.

She didn't understand his frown or thinly compressed lips. 'Fine. Let's get this evening over and done with.'

'Sounds good to me,' she said, half wishing they'd revert to sparring.

She liked light-hearted Cash. Grumpy Cash, not so much, especially when she had a feeling she'd been the cause of his sudden mood.

Thirty minutes later, after dancing to another ten power ballads amid couples jostling for prime dance-floor space, Lucy yearned for a hot chocolate and a warm bed. A bed without Cash in it, despite her treacherous memory replaying that scorching dance-floor kiss at will.

Thankfully, he hadn't tried a repeat despite the cameras filtering through the couples and shooting random snippets.

Didn't matter, because every time his hand grazed her hip or touched her waist she remembered. The heat. The skill. The all-consuming desire of being kissed by him; and left wanting more.

'You okay?' He tipped her chin up as the last strains of *Bette Davis Eyes* faded.

She nodded. 'Just tired.'

And incredibly drained. It was hard faking it—and to think this was only the first event.

'Come on, I'll walk you out.' He slid an arm around her waist, solicitous and caring, almost as lethal a combination as his devilish, teasing side.

Heck, who was she kidding? After their session on the dance floor she'd find him singing the national anthem appealing.

However, their escape was thwarted by the approach of one of the organisers brandishing an electronic tablet.

'You two are gold,' he said, flipping the screen towards them. 'That footage of you earlier? It's had over a thousand votes in thirty minutes.'

Lucy almost asked 'what footage' but she didn't need to, as with a sinking heart she watched her sizzling lip lock with Cash replayed in sharp, pixelated colour.

'You're in the lead by a mile.' The guy beamed like a benevolent father. 'Keep up the good work and you'll win top prize for sure.'

As the guy strode away Cash turned to her, took one look at her face, and guided her towards the door.

'Did you see that?' she hissed, embarrassment warring with anger, the latter winning out. 'That clip needed an X rating.'

'Too right.'

Lucy heard a hint of amusement beneath the pride in his tone, an inflection that made her head snap up to see an ear-splitting grin.

'You think this is funny?' she shrieked, hating how shrewish she sounded, hating this out-of-control feeling more.

'I think it's pretty damn hot.' He touched her bottom lip, tracing its contour, making her yearn for him all over again.

But she *couldn't* want Cash. He had heartbreaker written all over him and she had no intention of offering her heart to any guy ever again.

'Lucy?'

She frowned and his fingertip drifted up to smooth the dent between her brows.

'It's no big deal, being attracted to each other. We're adults. We're single.' His appreciative gaze drifted over her. 'And you're smoking hot. Stands to reason we're going to get carried away occasionally.'

The only thing that resonated from his altruistic speech

was the fact he found her smoking hot. And, however much she tried to dismiss his compliments, she loved hearing them. She'd been starved for compliments for a long time, and as the protective barrier around her icy heart thawed a little she knew her defences were at risk of melting completely.

The more time she spent with him, the greater the danger. Which meant she needed to keep things strictly professional.

She stepped back, putting some much-needed distance between them. 'Forget it. I need to get home and put the finishing touches on your quote.'

If he noticed the enforced chill he didn't call her on it. 'No worries.'

But as he held her coat so she could slip into it Lucy had plenty of worries. The main one centred on the guy who was slowly but surely charming his way into her life.

'Not so fast, lovebirds.' Raoul, the PR firm's marketing whiz in charge of this week, wriggled his way between Lucy and Cash and linked elbows with them. 'That public pash was gold so why don't we capitalise on the hype and do your private interview now?'

Lucy swallowed a groan. The last thing she felt like doing now was being asked a bunch of questions she'd probably stuff up because she was still inwardly reeling from Cash's kiss.

She needed time to regroup. And she was still craving that mega hot chocolate—the only thing that stood a chance of drowning the butterflies still fluttering madly in her belly.

Cash cast a quick glance her way and shook his head. 'Maybe another time, Raoul?'

Touched by Cash's intuition, she smiled her gratitude and he winked back.

But Raoul didn't have the same sensitivity to her need for a break and he bustled them towards a small VIP room. 'Surely you want to win this thing by capitalising on the hype after that kiss?'

To Lucy's dismay, they couldn't back out of this no matter how much she wanted to postpone. They had to make this look as authentic as possible for Cash's sake and appearing recalcitrant at their first event would raise suspicion.

By Cash's sudden frown, he'd come to the same conclusion, so she conveyed her agreement with a slight nod.

Cash raised an eyebrow, clarifying she was sure, and she once again appreciated his thoughtfulness for her feelings.

Buoyed by being so cared for, she squared her shoulders and nodded. 'Let's do this.'

'Brilliant,' Raoul said, beckoning to one of the lurking camera crew. 'Trust me, this'll be fun.'

With his gel-slicked hair, beady eyes and over-effusiveness, Raoul would be the last person Lucy would trust. On the upside, she'd been dreading this stupid one-on-one interview and the faster she got it out of the way, the better.

Cash grimaced behind Raoul's back and she stifled a giggle.

While Raoul fussed around a purple suede sofa, rearranging cushions and ordering the camera crew around, Cash slid his arm around her waist and ducked down to murmur in her ear, 'You sure you want to do this now?'

His concern unnerved her as much as his proximity. 'Yeah. Faster we finish, faster we can get out of here.'

'I like the way you think,' he said, his fingers skating

across her hip and making her bite her bottom lip to stop a moan escaping. 'I also like the way you kissed me back there.'

'Stop it.' She elbowed him, chuckling when he exhaled in an oomph. 'Aren't you the slightest bit concerned we may stuff up our answers here?'

'Nope. When in doubt, fake it.'

'We're doing a good job of that,' she said, glancing over her shoulder to ensure no one could listen in.

'Not all of it's fake,' he said, staring at her lips so she couldn't mistake his insinuation. 'That kiss? Memorably real.'

'Stop talking about it.' She tried to elbow him again but he laughed and dodged. 'You're rattling me.'

'Rattling is good.' He smirked. 'Means you care.'

'Do not.' She tilted her nose in the air, instantly regretting her defiance when he kissed the tip.

'Yeah, you do.' His wicked grin snatched her breath. 'It's okay, you know, to admit you find me irresistible.'

Lucy had no intention of admitting anything of the sort, however true it was. Falling for a guy too fast was the fatal flaw that had led her down the disastrous relationship path before; no way in hell would she make the same mistake again.

'Okay, I'll go first.' Without breaking eye contact, he said, 'I like you.'

Some of her resistance to Cash melted in the face of his abject honesty. Yet the longer he stared at her with that beguiling mix of charm and confidence, the more her doubts grew.

The guy had coerced her into posing as his girlfriend for a week. He schmoozed for a living. Could this be a deliberate ploy to soften her up so she gave a great interview to further his cause?

'I like me too,' she said, deliberately flippant as she eased away from him and sat on the sofa.

A small frown creased his brow, as if she'd confused or annoyed him in some way. But when Raoul returned to fussing over them rather than the props, Cash sat next to her and assumed a laid-back slouch as if he didn't have a care in the world.

Yeah, he must've been playing her. Because a guy like him didn't 'like' a girl like her in a few days. Life didn't work that way. She should know.

'Ready to roll?' Raoul drew up a footstool out of camera range and perched on it like a hyper parrot, all fluffing feathers and flapping wings. 'I'll ask you each a set of random questions regarding romance and you answer with the first thing that pops into your head.'

Uh-oh. The first words popping into Lucy's head right now weren't fit to be said let alone broadcast on YouTube.

'Keep it simple, folks. Short responses. Funny is good.' Raoul clapped his hands. 'Right, we're ready to roll.' He held up a hand at the cameraman and counted down three, two, one with his fingers.

The camera panned to Raoul and he flashed a dazzling smile. 'Good evening. We're live at the eighties disco tonight with the couple of the moment, Cash Burgess and Lucy Grant.'

Raoul crooked a finger at the camera, as if he was inviting them into a private session where he'd reveal deep, dark secrets. *As long as the secret wasn't that their relationship was a big fat fake*, Lucy thought.

'So what would you like to know about this intriguing couple? Me? I'm all about the romance.' Raoul swivelled towards Cash, and Lucy released the breath she'd been inadvertently holding. 'Tell us, Cash. Was it love at first sight for you and Lucy?'

Cash swallowed as Lucy broke out in a sweat. Hell, these questions were going to be sheer and utter torture.

To his credit, Cash settled deeper into the sofa and draped an arm across the back of it, his fingertips skating along her shoulder, the epitome of relaxed when he had to be feeling as uptight as her.

'While Lucy is incredibly gorgeous and could tempt any sane man to fall in love with her at first sight, I'd like to think it was her other qualities that intrigued me from the start.'

Raoul blinked, as if surprised by Cash's answer, as Lucy wished her stupid heart weren't leaping all over the place at the apparent sincerity behind his words.

None of this was real, she reminded herself. But for a fleeting moment, hearing Cash speak supposedly from the heart, she wished it were.

Raoul turned to her. 'What about you, Lucy? Love at first sight?'

'More like insta-lust,' she deadpanned, while pointedly staring Cash up and down.

Raoul laughed as she'd hoped, while Cash pinned her with an all-too-fiery gaze that promised of payback later.

'Your idea of the perfect Saturday night?' Raoul pointed at Cash and the camera zoomed in.

'Too easy.' Cash dragged his gaze away from her to focus on the camera. 'Taking Lucy to dinner at Melbourne's finest restaurant, theatre or jazz club after, finishing with cocktails on the thirty-fifth floor of my favourite hotel.'

Raoul looked suitably impressed. Maybe he should date Cash for the week.

'Lucy, how about you?'

Lucy linked her hands and rested them on her knees.

'Cosy night in. A classic old black and white movie. Popcorn. Soda. Chocolate. Whipped cream. Cash…'

Cash's gaze snapped to hers again and she could've sworn the air between them sizzled.

Okay, she wasn't playing fair, trying to get him back for that kiss on the dance floor, but this was what he wanted, right? For the kissing couple to demonstrate how hot they were for each other?

Raoul fanned his face. 'Phew, we can see why this guy is smitten with you, Lucy.' He swung back to Cash. 'Favourite romantic song?'

'Anything that gets Lucy to kiss me like she did on the dance floor.'

Touché. Lucy should've expected Cash to fire back.

Raoul smirked. 'Lucy, what's yours?'

'Moves Like Jagger.'

Expecting her to say more, Raoul frowned. 'Why?'

'Because Cash has the moves…and how.' She winked at the camera, startled to discover she was actually enjoying hamming it up.

Raoul wolf-whistled while Cash's sexy smirk promised retribution. 'I could keep asking questions all night but we have a few other couples to interview, so, to wind up, why don't you both finish by telling me: what's your idea of the perfect date?'

Lucy gestured at Cash to go first, a dramatic arm sweep that had Cash grinning. 'Flying interstate for a naughty weekend.'

Raoul nodded his approval. 'Anywhere in particular?'

'Preferably somewhere scorching hot, so Lucy parades around in the skimpiest clothes imaginable,' Cash said, sliding closer to her on the sofa and leaving her no option but to snuggle into his shoulder.

She'd kill him.

She was fine firing back sassy barbs with some distance between them, but, with his spicy aftershave enveloping her in a sensual cloud and his body radiating enough heat to make her melt on the spot, she was sure to stuff up this next answer.

'What's your perfect date, Lucy?' Raoul made a circular motion with his hand to indicate they had to wind it up and she rushed into her answer.

'Low key. Simple. From the heart,' she said, instantly regretting her honesty when Cash eased back to look at her face. 'A picnic with my favourite foods. A mountain top. Intimacy.'

Cash held her gaze and she couldn't look away no matter how much she wanted to. The public would lap this up, seeing it as a very private moment between lovers. When in fact Cash was staring at her as if he could see all the way down to her soul. As if he knew this was the first honest thing she'd said all night. And he appreciated it.

So she added, 'With a man who makes me want to devour him more than the food.'

'Love it.' Raoul clapped his hands again, obviously pleased with the results of the interview. 'Thanks, Lucy and Cash. We wish you all the best in your quest to win GR8 4U Public Relations' Most Romantic Valentine's Day Couple.'

As Raoul beckoned to the camera crew to follow him and find the next poor couple, Lucy slumped into the sofa, belatedly realising Cash still cuddled her close and she'd inadvertently slumped into him.

'You did good,' he murmured, hugging her.

'Raoul seemed to lap up our lies, that's the main thing,' she said, allowing the brief comfort of being warmed by his embrace before standing. 'I'm beat. Time to go.'

'Not so fast.' Cash stood and laid a hand on her fore-arm. 'You gave some interesting answers.'

Lucy shrugged, determined to play down how much she'd loved sparring with him and the resultant buzz. 'You heard what Raoul said. The public lap up that sort of stuff.'

'So you were just giving the public what they wanted to hear, huh?' Cash's fingers slid around her wrist and he tried to tug her closer.

She resisted. 'Absolutely.'

'So all that talk of insta-lust and whipped cream and devouring me was just you playing the part of a smit-ten girlfriend?'

'Yep.' If she nodded any harder her head would fall off.

'Pity.' He finally released her wrist when she wouldn't give in. 'I'm sure I could rustle up some popcorn and chocolate in my pantry. And we could save the whipped cream for—'

'I'm allergic to dairy,' she blurted, desperate to get away before the heat flushing her body stained her cheeks crimson.

He laughed. 'You're good at fibbing for the cameras, sweetheart, but I can pick when you're lying a mile off.'

'Bull,' she said, making the mistake of sneaking a glance at him.

Cash swooped in for a quick peck on the lips before straightening, his smug expression alerting her to the fact she hadn't fooled him at all.

'Tonight was a resounding success,' he said, offer-ing her a hand that she ignored. 'And the best part? We made out.'

'What are you, twelve?'

He laughed harder, slipped an arm around her waist and guided her towards the door. 'I'm looking forward to seeing what you come up with next for the rest of the week.'

As long as it wasn't more of that unexpected honesty that had popped out at the end of the interview, Lucy was safe.

For now.

CHAPTER EIGHT

ONE OF THE perks of Cash's job was the long lunches, where he took his clients to Melbourne's top restaurants and spent a leisurely few hours wining and dining and talking figures.

He thrived on it, taking the fortunes of his famous clientele and making them more money.

Not today. Today, he was off his game and it made him edgy and crappy and cranky.

Not good enough, considering the woman sitting opposite him was Australia's top talk-show host at the moment. Cecilia Boyle was eloquent, intelligent and gorgeous. A tall, willowy blonde, she was just his type. The type of woman to tempt him to mix business with pleasure.

Not something he set out to do but it had been a perk of the job on occasion. Never instigated by him, and he chose his dalliances wisely, ensuring they both knew the outcome going in. Commitment-free. No long-term involvement.

It was the reason he was in this mess in the first place, his radar alerting him to the desperate starlet wanting to sleep her way into his portfolio.

He'd rejected her, she'd started rumours and here he was, with a fake girlfriend for a week.

A fake girlfriend who was the reason behind his edginess.

Lucy Grant was one giant distraction and, after last night, he couldn't get her out of his head.

She was the reason he was off his game today. And it pissed him off even more, the fact he was letting last night interfere with his business today.

'I like the asset distribution you've suggested,' Cecilia said, her voice lowering as she touched his arm. 'Do you want to discuss it further at my place?'

Cash should've been tempted. He should've taken one look at the sexy blonde in the figure-hugging cobalt jersey dress and escorted her from the restaurant to her apartment.

Instead, he flashed his best appeasing smile and eased away. 'Thanks, but I've got back-to-back meetings all day.'

Her smile froze, the hard glint in her eyes the only sign her ego had taken a hit, before her acting skills kicked in and her expression blanked. 'Not a problem. I'll look over your suggestions this afternoon and email you my choices by tonight.'

'Sounds good.' They shook hands, brief and perfunctory, and he breathed a sigh of relief. Relief that was short-lived when Cecilia left the restaurant and he was left to mull.

Not that he needed to ponder much. Lucy Grant had him in a tailspin and, for a guy who prided himself on cool detachment when it came to the fairer sex, he was in way over his head with this one.

And with six more days to get through without letting Lucy get further under his skin than she already had, it looked like things were set to get even more distracting. Annoyed by his wayward thoughts, Cash flipped his laptop open to enter notes from the meeting with Cecilia, when a shadow fell over his table.

'If it isn't Casanova,' Bart said, slipping onto the seat Cecilia had vacated. 'Nice show you put on last night.'

'Good PR,' Cash said, not wanting to discuss his out-of-control reaction to Lucy with his mate. 'Voters are lapping it up apparently.'

'And you've bumped the story with Psycho Girl onto page six while your lip-lock with the hot gardener is page three in the social pages.'

'Great,' Cash said, typing a few addendums before glancing up. 'Not that we're aiming for the big prize, but, out of curiosity, what is it?'

Bart tsk-tsked. 'Weren't you paying attention at the introductory session?'

No, he'd been too busy picking his jaw up off the floor when Lucy had strutted into that room, flaunting her new image.

'Just tell me already.'

'Valentine's Day dream date. Limo pick up. Drive to Mornington Peninsula. Dinner at an exclusive winery.' Bart winked. 'With an indulgent stay over in five-star luxury.'

Cash's pulse quickened at the phrase 'stay over'. The thought of having Lucy all to himself was enough to send his mind spinning all over again. The sexual tension between them when they'd danced, their manic make-out session...would equate to fireworks in the bedroom.

Bart tilted his head, studying him. 'For a guy who is doing this for the PR, you're sure giving a good impression of a guy who's besotted.'

Cash shrugged, determined to play down how connected he felt. 'Lucy's a nice girl. We get on okay.'

Bart sniggered. 'If that kiss was any indication, saying

you *get on okay* is understatement of the year.' He tapped at his smartphone and turned the screen to face Cash. 'And have you seen the interview you did later? Sizzling.'

'You know none of this is real,' Cash said, deliberately averting his gaze from Bart's phone.

Because the truth was, he'd watched that interview three times when he'd got home last night, fascinated by Lucy's many sides.

She'd been bold and sassy one minute, hamming it up for his benefit, but her response to the last question had thrown him.

For the first time all interview she'd appeared uncertain, unguarded, as if all that stuff about a private picnic on a mountaintop was coming from somewhere more sincere than her other answers.

And he'd had the damndest reaction to her honesty... he'd wanted to take her on her dream date immediately.

He chided himself. It was pointless and stupid, reading too much into Lucy's responses to him last night. They had roles to play and that was what they were doing.

He of all people should know how brilliant women could be at acting. Hadn't his mum given a sterling performance as maternal caregiver for a few years, before showing her true colours and turfing him out?

Bart stared at the screen on his phone and wolf-whistled. 'You've got some serious chemistry going on there.'

'Showmanship for the cameras,' Cash said, making a grand show of looking at his watch. 'Speaking of which, I've got a ton of work to finish if I'm to make that riverside picnic tomorrow.'

Another function, another chance to spend time with Lucy. It would be laughable, how much he was looking forward to seeing her, if it weren't so downright pathetic.

Cash didn't pine over women. Although, considering

he couldn't get Lucy out of his head and was counting down the hours until tomorrow, it seemed he was doing exactly that. What was it about this particular woman that had him feeling so vulnerable?

Bart slapped him on the back. 'My money's on you taking out the grand prize and getting the girl.'

For an irrational second, Cash almost wished Bart's prediction were right.

Lucy thrived on manic mornings. Up at six, out of the door by six-thirty, mulching her first garden of the day by seven. She loved dawn frosts and crisp air and dew on the grass. She loved tackling the hardest tasks first. But most of all, she loved the solitude of working in a garden surrounded by earthy smells and the chirping of birds.

She relished the peace. Found solace in it.

Except today, when the tranquillity merely served to make her thoughts more insistent and exceptionally loud.

This morning had been busier than most. She'd mowed four lawns, trimmed eight hedges and manicured three flowerbeds.

Yet all the vigorous physical activity in the world couldn't take her mind off this afternoon.

A romantic picnic with Cash.

She'd been up half the night, determinedly ignoring what had happened at the disco and focusing on the one thing bound to subdue her attraction: designing his new garden.

Concentrating on work would keep her desire for Cash at bay and reinforce why she was spending time with him in the first place.

For the money. Cold, hard cash that would save Gram's house. As opposed to warm, hard Cash, who would destroy the independent life she'd built for herself.

Not that it was his fault she'd been going through a man drought and was crushing on the first hot guy to enter her sphere.

Ironically, given that she was only here for the money, she wouldn't have minded if he'd been a gardener or a tradesmen or any other blue-collar worker. She could handle those guys. It was confident, suave, wealthy guys in suits she had trouble with.

On the upside, she'd compiled a succinct yet inspired quote for Cash's garden.

The downside? She'd have to work there, which meant seeing the guy way too often over the next few weeks once this Valentine's Day rubbish was finished.

As she shrugged into a pale pink cashmere sweater her gaze landed on his garden's plans spread across her dining table.

She loved it. Loved the quintessential Aussie theme she'd gone for. The high limestone wall in the far corner, with inlaid mosaics designed by indigenous artists. The granite edging and pebble paving near the five-foot water feature ending in a pond. The sculpture wall featuring imprinted marsupials. The spectacular flowering Golden Lyre grevillea. The stunning crimson Callistemon Firebrand bottlebrush. The delicate Chenille Honeymyrtle and majestic Candlestick banksia and perky yellow Knobthorn acacia.

She'd co-ordinated plants and colours with minute attention to detail, loving how her designs came to life beneath her fingertips, first as a sketch, later on computer.

It had been easier than the usual design process of site analysis, where she'd spend hours taking measurements, photos and noting existing vegetation, because she already knew every inch of the space she'd be working with.

Though she had spent an inordinate time on the concept plan, ensuring the scaled layout of his new garden would wow.

When she'd finished, he'd have a garden people would admire and talk about. And, in turn, ensure her business boomed so she could set up that nest egg for Gram and herself.

She never wanted to feel insecure or at the mercy of a guy again, after Adrian had made her feel both. Walking away from his fortune had been easy. Making it on her own had been tough. But she'd done it, and the faster she financially secured her and Gram's future, the better.

In a way, Gram's misfortune had opened her eyes. If someone you loved that much could leave you vulnerable, who could you really trust?

She'd like to think she could trust again some day. She wasn't a bitter and twisted divorcee who'd never tread down the committed-relationship path again. But if she did ever take a chance on trusting again, she'd make damn sure she had her own assets protected and money to fall back on.

Her mobile phone beeped as she locked the front door and one glance at the screen made her heart race in anticipation. Cash Burgess was a client so it stood to reason she had his number in her mobile. She stored all her clients' numbers. Yet by the timing of this text message, she had a feeling this wasn't business.

She stabbed at the icon to bring up her messages.

Did U pack ur teddy?

Confused, Lucy reread the message, before getting the picnic allusion.

Her thumb flew over the keypad:

Not a teddy bear's picnic, tho I'm in a grizzly mood.

She hit send as she slid into her car, hoping she could get through this afternoon unscathed—and without Cash surprising her with any more sizzling lip-locks.

Her phone pinged again.

Who's talking about bears?

It took her a second to absorb the innuendo behind his message and she had an instant image of her wearing a sheer black teddy and Cash ripping it off her. With his teeth.

'Damn it,' she muttered, trying to think up a suitable response and coming up empty.

She settled for a sedate and rather pathetic '*C U soon*'.

And spent the next twenty minutes driving from her place to the picnic spot on the Yarra River near the Botanical Gardens trying to ignore the far from sedate visions of the two of them together that were flooding her imagination.

'You'd better be on your best behaviour today,' Lucy said, glaring at Cash over a chilled glass of chardonnay as they sat on their cosy picnic rug for two. 'And that means no kissing.'

'Spoilsport,' he said, raising his glass in her direction. 'Haven't you heard? That's what couples in love do in the lead up to Valentine's Day.'

He blew her a kiss for good measure. 'And that one doesn't count.'

She smiled, unable to resist his teasing. Scooting a little closer to him so they wouldn't be overheard, she murmured, 'Do you think we're the only ones here who think Valentine's Day is a load of codswallop?'

He grinned and jerked his head towards the couple on his left: a couple currently sipping their wine with arms entwined. 'Not them.'

He rolled his eyes towards the right, where a guy hand-fed chocolate-dipped strawberries to his girlfriend. 'Or them.'

He stared at the couple directly in front of them, with the woman sitting on the guy's lap while she nipped his earlobe. 'And they're positively sickening.'

'Couldn't agree more.' She clinked her glass to his. 'Here's to being a couple of anti-cupids.'

'I'll drink to that.'

Lucy could do this. Could joke and laugh and pretend she wasn't on the banks of the Yarra River, surrounded by liveried waiters serving exquisite picnic food, topping up their glasses, with a bunch of soppy couples who actually believed all the romantic claptrap Valentine's Day perpetuated.

He lowered his glass, studying her with an intensity she found unnerving. 'Can I ask you something?'

'Sure. Doesn't mean I'll answer you.'

The corners of his mouth quirked. 'Why are you such a cynic?'

'Could ask you the same thing.'

He hesitated, as if weighing up his response, before placing his glass on a mini-tray and leaning back on his hands, arms outstretched. 'My mum chucked us out when I was little. Wrecked my old man.'

He stared at the river, lost in memories she wished she hadn't intruded on. 'She was rich. Dabbling with a rough-around-the-edges guy. Probably got tired of Dad. Or me. Whatever. Dad changed from an easy-going, happy guy into a stern, taciturn grump. We had no money. Nothing I did was good enough. Until I hit my teens and started bringing in the money by working part-time jobs.' He shook his head. 'Was the only time I ever saw Dad without a frown, when I brought in those regular paycheques.'

Lucy stared at the guy she'd pegged for rich and shallow initially, stunned by his hidden depths. And feeling incredibly guilty for judging him.

'I'm sorry.' The trite apology tripped from her lips and she instantly wished she could take it back.

How many friends—in reality acquaintances—had offered the required 'sorry' when they'd learned of her divorce from Adrian? And she'd accepted each and every one with grace, not blurting the truth despite wanting to. Most of her friends back then had been Adrian's friends and she'd wanted to leave that world behind without tarnishing what she'd once had.

Pity her ex-husband hadn't had the same compunction.

'Don't be, I'm over it.' Cash shrugged, as if his admission meant nothing. But she noticed the tension in his shoulders, in the fine lines fanning his eyes, and wished she'd kept her mouth shut. 'Fact of life, not everyone gets the fairy tale. End of story.'

'Tell me about it,' she said, the admission tripping from her lips in a moment of shared weakness. A moment she instantly regretted when he quirked an eyebrow.

'Sounds like you have a story of your own to tell, Miss Grant.'

'Not really.'

Last thing she felt like doing was sharing her disastrous marriage to Adrian with a virtual stranger.

His signature wicked grin was back, potent and persuasive. 'I showed you mine. Least you can do is show me yours.'

Lucy looked into Cash's deep blue eyes. Eyes without shadows or hurt. Eyes without secrets.

How did he do that? Forgive so easily? Move on from a past that sounded sad at best, heartbreaking at worst.

She might have moved on but she could never forgive Adrian.

'How did you forgive your folks?'

Puzzled, he searched her face for clarity. 'What do you mean?'

She plucked at a serviette, shredding it. 'Sounds like you had it tough. Your mum rejected you. Your dad shut down emotionally. How do you move on from something like that?'

'Focus on the stuff you can count on.'

'Like?'

'Money. Hard work. Success.'

She could identify with the hard work. The other two? Not so much.

'So who can't you forgive?' He stilled her fiddling fingers and slid the serviette away, covering her hand with his. As their hands made contact she was warmed by a tiny flicker of comfort.

She tried to dismiss the sudden closeness. She didn't want to tell him. She didn't want to open herself up like that.

But his touch was firm and warm, his expression was understanding and empathic, and she found herself blabbing before she could stop.

'I was married nine years ago. Blissfully happy for twelve months, before discovering the bastard cheated on me. Repeatedly. With more than one woman.' Her forced laugh sounded slightly hysterical. 'How cliché is that?'

He squeezed her hand and held on tighter. 'I could say

I'm sorry but I'd be lying. The way I see it? That prick did me a favour.'

He lifted her hand to his lips and brushed a soft kiss across her knuckles. 'Because you wouldn't be here with me now if you were still married to that moron, so screw him.'

Some of Lucy's residual bitterness faded as the skin across her knuckles tingled from Cash's kiss. 'True. How lucky are we, indulging in a fake relationship for individual gain?'

He frowned at her sarcasm. 'Hey, don't do that.' He cupped her cheek and for a crazy moment she wanted to lean into him. 'We all do what we have to do to get by. And whatever the reason is that you're putting up with me for a week? It must be important.'

Damn, if he didn't stop being so understanding, Lucy would start bawling any second. And she never cried.

'It is,' she said, too abrupt if the shadows clouding his eyes were any indication. 'Now can we get back to polishing off the rest of the baby quiche and smoked salmon tartlets before those deluded amorous couples come up for air and scoff the lot?'

He nodded and held out his hand to her as he stood. 'Let's skip the waiters in penguin suits and go raid the gourmet hamper then come back here and stuff our faces silly.'

'Lead the way.' She placed her hand in his, allowing him to pull her to her feet.

In doing so, he tugged a little too hard and she stumbled against him. Deliciously close. Not close enough.

'Oops. Sorry,' he said, with a wink, a moment before he kissed her. A soft, teasing graze of his lips against hers. A wistful kiss that made her yearn for more.

'I thought we agreed on no kissing,' she said, trying to frown and failing miserably.

'That wasn't a kiss. It was a "let's forget our crappy pasts and have a good time today" friendly gesture.'

'I suggest for the rest of the afternoon you keep those *friendly gestures* to yourself.' She bumped him with her hip, enjoying his comical mock outrage. 'Agreed?'

'We'll see,' he said, casually slinging his arm across her shoulders as if it was the most natural thing in the world as they headed for the gourmet picnic goodies laid out in individual hampers.

Cash was incorrigible. But thanks to the revelations they'd shared, he was also fast becoming incredibly appealing on more than just a physical level.

Lucy really hoped the organisers had stocked loads of chocolate in that basket, because she was in dire need of a major sugar fix.

Anything to take her mind off how utterly, incredibly gorgeous her fake boyfriend was, and how he'd somehow managed to get her talking about her past.

She needed to be extra careful around Cash for the rest of the week. Because she had a feeling the more confidences shared, the more *friendly gestures*, the higher the risk to her insulated heart.

Asking Lucy back to his place after the picnic had been a dumb idea. Sure, Cash had couched it in terms of going over the plans for his garden, but he knew deep down it had much more to do with her company than her plans for his flowerbeds.

They'd connected at the picnic, on a far deeper level than he'd anticipated or wanted.

Why the hell had he blurted all that stuff about his

past? He'd never told anyone about his folks, especially not women he dated.

Though technically he wasn't dating Lucy. And she was a good listener, with an uncanny knack of delving beneath his cocky façade. It wasn't something he deliberately did, presenting a confident front, but something he'd acquired over the years; a natural extension of himself.

He'd learned it young, when he had to pretend his dad's callous indifference and mood swings didn't matter. And later, when the only time Dad could crack a smile was when he handed over his pay cheque.

Cash had hated those crappy part-time jobs. While the rest of his teenage mates had been skylarking in the city or hanging out at the local games arcade or chasing girls, he'd been busting his ass working three jobs: newspaper deliveries before school, butcher's assistant after school and waiter at a local restaurant most nights.

Thankfully he'd had a knack for figures too, and had completed an accelerated maths programme that had carried over into university.

Cash had liked making money, had liked seeing his father happy when he'd brought it home. He never knew his mum, and never wanted to, though he guessed he owed her for inadvertently launching his career in the entertainment business.

He'd seen her at a theatre premiere once, not long after he'd graduated uni, recognising her from the sole picture his dad kept hidden in a sock drawer.

She'd been hanging off some wealthy guy, the glitter of her diamonds matching the glint from his gold Rolex. With the foyer full, bouncers started turning people away, and that was when she glanced over her shoulder, saw him and froze.

Cash never knew what alerted her to the fact he was

her son—probably because he was the spitting image of his dad—but something must've given away his lineage because she strutted up to the bouncer, whispered something in his ear and the next thing Cash knew he was being ushered in.

She disappeared into the crowd and Cash searched for her out of curiosity more than a will to thank her. What kind of a woman booted her own child out and left him with no money when she had enough to burn?

He'd often wondered if she'd offered them money and his father's wounded pride had prevented him from taking it, but hadn't wanted to stir up his dad's anger by asking.

Not that it mattered. His mother hadn't wanted him. A fact he'd accepted a long time ago. And by her one small action that night, he'd met a few B-list celebrities, had given some free financial advice over cocktails, and his career as an advisor to the stars had been born.

On the odd occasion, usually around Mother's Day, when colleagues were buying exorbitant flower bouquets and perfume for their mums, he'd experience a pang. A twinge that maybe he should've been proactive in establishing a bond between them and getting to know her.

Then he'd remember his dad's drinking binges and irrational fury and lifelong bitterness, and the urge would dissipate.

Cash was happy with his life. Easy. Comfortable. Uncomplicated.

Until Lucy padded back into the lounge room, her purple-painted toenails sparkling in the down lights, and he realised just how complicated his life was becoming.

'Here you go.' She placed a glass of water next to her plans spread on the coffee table and sat on the floor, cross-legged. 'So what do you think of your new garden?'

'It's brilliant,' he said, meaning it. Her plans to transform his garden were nothing short of inspired. Then again, she could've sketched a bunch of stick-figure trees and he wouldn't have cared.

All he could think about was how good he felt when she was around. And how he'd like to prolong the feeling.

Crazy, considering he didn't even know her.

Yet he'd shared a very private piece of his life with her today and she'd reciprocated. Stood to reason they'd grow a little closer over the week. But this strange, out-of-control feeling whenever she was around?

Not good.

'You really like it?' The hint of vulnerability begged him to place a hand on her shoulder and squeeze.

'I'm not usually in the habit of saying things I don't mean.' He slipped off the couch and sat next to her on the floor, his hand skating across the back of her neck so that his arm ended up draped across her shoulders. 'You're extremely talented. This garden will be worth every cent you extort out of me when it's done.'

She elbowed him in the ribs. 'Hey! I'm worth it.'

'Yes, you are,' he said, his smile fading as she glanced up, their faces temptingly close.

Cash had no idea how long they sat there, staring at each other. His heart pounded so hard he thought it'd leap out of his chest, that was how much he wanted her.

He wanted to kiss her.

Hell, he wanted to do a lot more than kiss.

He waited for Lucy to shrug off his arm, leap up and put an end to this ridiculously tension-fraught moment while the air practically sizzled between them.

His fingers grazed her bare upper arm, the soft skin warm and inviting.

She didn't flinch or pull away.

He traced lazy circles, his fingertips snagging on the armhole of her tank top.

She didn't move.

His hand drifted towards her neck, slowly rubbing, an impromptu massage that bordered on erotic.

Lucy's eyelids fluttered shut at the same time her lips parted, allowing a soft, wistful moan to escape.

It was all the invitation he needed.

He kissed her.

Ravaged her mouth with the pent-up frustration making him want to tear her clothes off.

Taunted her with his tongue. His turn to groan when she matched him.

She surged upward. Straddled him. Made him go a little nuts when she devoured him right back.

He strummed her back, and lower, to cup her ass.

She tore her mouth from his, staring at him in wide-eyed wonder. 'What the hell are we doing?'

'About to have mind-blowing sex because we like each other?'

'I don't like you,' she said, her coy smile making a mockery of her feisty declaration.

'Too bad. Because I really like you.' He ground his pelvis against her to prove it. 'And I intend to show you how much all night long.'

'Is that more of your usual overconfidence talking?'

'Guess you'll have to stick around to find out.' He nuzzled her neck, inhaling the subtle, sweet fragrance that was pure Lucy.

When she didn't respond, he raised his head to look her in the eye. Last thing he needed was to complicate their weeklong arrangement. He knew the score about tonight. No-holds-barred sex. Did Lucy?

'Last chance, Luce.' He searched her beautiful brown

eyes for a hint of regret, relieved when he only saw excitement and passion and heat. 'If you stay, I'm going to ravish you all night. If you leave, nothing changes. Up to you.'

She clambered off his lap and he silently cursed giving her an out.

'Decisions, decisions,' she said, with her back turned to him.

Cash didn't show vulnerability to anyone but in that moment he had to say what was in his heart. 'I want you to stay.'

Lucy didn't speak, the silence taut with frustration and unfulfilled desire.

Then she slowly turned back. Extended her hand to him. Her lips curved in a teasing smile. Her eyes bright. 'Then I'll stay,' she said as he placed his hand in hers and she pulled him to his feet.

The simplicity of her acceptance caught him off guard and he hugged her tight, wondering where the weird emotional stuff burning his chest was coming from and wishing it would go the hell away.

Lucy slid her hands between their bodies and rested her palms on his chest, gently easing them apart. 'You're not getting all sentimental on me, are you?'

Stupidly, he was, and he had no idea why. Something about this woman—her inherent goodness, her guilelessness, her honesty—got to him.

So he did the one thing guaranteed to re-establish control.

Wrapped his arms around her waist, hoisted her up, and backed her up against the nearest wall.

She laughed. She actually laughed, a genuinely happy sound that made him feel like a god.

'Just for the record? I love hearing you laugh, but when

it's right before we're going to…you know…my manhood could take offence.'

She laughed harder and he found himself grinning right back.

'Manhood? Seriously? Is that what you call it?'

To his immense surprise, he felt heat in his cheeks, as if he was about to blush. 'Well, I don't have a nickname for it, if that's what you're asking.'

'I'm teasing.' Her laughter subsided as she raised a hand to cup his cheek. 'You're the most confident, charming guy I've ever met and I like seeing you a little off guard.'

He could live with confident and charming. And her admiration.

For a fleeting second, he wondered what kind of a stupid bastard her ex-husband had been, to screw around on a woman of Lucy's calibre.

If she was this sweet now, he could only imagine she would've been even more innocent nine years ago.

But no point dwelling on the dumbass now. He had a reputation to uphold for Lucy. Confident and charming. Yeah, he could do both.

'You know the thing about teasing?' He pressed his pelvis against her, savouring the soft moan that escaped her luscious lips. 'I give it back in spades.'

He claimed her mouth. Possessive. Demanding. Relishing her frenzied response as she writhed against him.

He'd expected her to be a tad reticent, so her uninhibited responses stoked his fire further.

He supported her butt and rested it on a nearby hall table, wrenching his mouth from hers. 'Bedroom?'

'Here,' she said, her eyes not leaving his as she snagged the hem of her top and peeled it upwards.

He groaned, his gaze riveted to her pink lace bra, her nipples dark and protruding through the sheer fabric.

His mouth went dry as she snapped the button on her jeans, unzipped and shucked them lower, stepping out of them, to stand barefoot in that sexy bra and a matching lace thong.

Pale pink lace against ivory satin skin. Stunning.

'Want to see the rest?' She rested a hand on her hip and cocked it in a provocative stance that accentuated her feminine curves.

'Hell yeah.' He hoped he didn't drool as he said it.

She winked. 'You'll have to catch me first.'

Before his befuddled brain could process what she meant, she took off, darting towards the stairs. 'You want to play tag at a time like this?' he shouted after her retreating back. 'Because a man in my condition can't run.'

She paused on the second to top step and glanced over her shoulder, her teasing smile pure vixen. 'I'm taking that as a good sign.' Her sultry gaze slid over him, lingering on his groin. 'All night, you said?'

He sprinted towards the stairs. The faster he caught her, the faster he could have her naked and pliant and begging for more.

She squealed as he leapt the steps three at a time and she took off again, dodging to her right. He chuckled as she reached the end of the hallway and glanced around, indecisive.

'My bedroom's this way, in case you were wondering.' He jerked a thumb over his shoulder, in the opposite direction to where she stood, a vision in her underwear.

'Guess you've got me cornered then.'

He stalked towards her, slow, deliberate strides, unbuttoning his shirt along the way.

Her eyes widened as she watched him and when he

shrugged out of it and flung it on the nearest banister, her tongue darted out to moisten her bottom lip.

Damn, he wanted to do that. Kiss those lips all night long.

'Come here.' He crooked his finger, delighting in the way she openly ogled his chest.

'What'll you do if I obey?'

He pretended to think, before snapping his fingers. 'I'll take off my jeans.'

A spark of fire lit her eyes. 'That's a good start.'

He took his time with the button fly, undoing each button painstakingly slowly.

When he was done, he slid the jeans over his hips, edged them down his thighs, and kicked them off, sending them flying over the railing where they landed somewhere on the floor below.

'Now you're just showing off.' She stopped a foot away. So close. Not close enough.

'No, this would be showing off.' He took off his grey boxers, incredibly empowered when she stared at his erection in open-mouthed surprise.

'Well, I can see where your confidence comes from,' she said, something akin to awe in her low tone. 'And all I can say is lucky me.'

He grinned at her typical bluntness as he reached out, snagged her bra strap and tugged gently. 'One of us is still overdressed.'

'Show me your bedroom and I'll remedy that,' she said, her hungry gaze still roaming his body.

'This way.' He took her hand, liking the way it fit so perfectly in his.

When he'd suggested they spend the night together, he'd expected Lucy to bolt. He hadn't anticipated that she'd respond like this. Playful. Sexy. As if it was the most natural thing in the world.

And the way she was teasing him? Her uninhibited sprint up his stairs in her panties? A major surprise. And a total turn-on.

The women he'd been with in the past were either voracious man-eaters who took the lead and wanted hard and fast, or simpering, sly game players who submitted because they thought he wanted it that way.

What Cash really wanted was a woman who matched him in every way, a woman to keep him on his toes, a woman who made him laugh.

Right now, Lucy ticked all the boxes and, by their verbal foreplay, he knew the sex was going to be mind-blowing.

They paused at his bedroom door. How many women had he brought up here over the years, eager for a night of fun, not caring whether they stayed or not? Didn't say much about him as a man, though until this moment he'd never felt ashamed of the way he'd emotionally shut off from his entanglements. He liked complication-free sex. So why the tsunami of doubt swamping him now? Why the worry that he wouldn't be able to stay shut off this time; that the moment they entered his bedroom their pretend relationship would move into complicated territory?

'Having second thoughts?' She squeezed his hand.

He tugged her into the bedroom by way of an answer, kicked the door shut and backed her towards the bed, keeping his eyes fixed on hers. 'No second thoughts. Time to make good on my promise to ravish you all night.'

They stopped when the backs of her knees hit the bed, Lucy's expectant expression making him experience his second flash of doubt in as many minutes.

Cash hated expectations. Every time he'd seen his dad's disappointment in life growing up, he'd felt compelled to strive harder and work longer and be better.

It was why he set the bar high now in everything he did. And he was proud of his achievements.

But never had he experienced this desperate need to meet the expectations of a woman. And he guessed that these would be no ordinary expectations, just as Lucy was no ordinary woman.

She was a woman driven to drastic measures, like posing as his fake girlfriend for a week. She was vulnerable and strong, sassy and sweet, a bundle of contradictions he was just dying to disentangle. In short, she was unlike any woman he'd ever met before.

He saw the momentary concern in her eyes, and, determined to banish any doubts they both might harbour, he slid an arm around her waist, held her secure and toppled them onto the bed.

She laughed as they landed in a tangle of arms and legs, her joyful exuberance dampening the last of his doubts.

He wanted her. She wanted him. A night of explosive sex didn't have to complicate anything.

She rolled onto her side, her face inches from his. She studied him, as if imprinting every detail of this significant moment in her memory.

He knew the feeling. He wanted to remember this later, wanted to replay every playful moment, every erotic second.

He traced the tan line of the sleeveless tank tops she wore for work, his fingertip skating over the top of her breast, over her shoulder, where he deftly unhooked her bra with one hand.

'Clever party trick,' she said, her lips curving into a saucy smile.

'The first of many.' He winked and rolled her onto her back, removing the bra and flinging it away.

He kissed his way down her stomach until he reached her thong, deliberately snagging his teeth on the elastic.

Her hips arched off the bed a little as he caught the scrap of lace underwear in his mouth and lowered it inch by inch until she was gloriously naked.

'Wow,' he said, filled with awe to see this incredible woman lying before him.

She wasn't self-conscious or uncomfortable. She was magnificent, and when she opened her arms to him he didn't need to be asked twice.

'You're beautiful,' he murmured, a moment before he kissed her, savouring the pleasure of lying body to body, skin to skin.

However, as their kisses deepened to carnal she writhed beneath him, threatening his hold on his self-control.

Leaving her lips with reluctance, he kissed along her jaw, her collarbone, her breasts. Taking his time to suck and lick and tease her nipples, her panted cries of encouragement stoking his fire further.

He nipped the tender undersides of her breasts.

He nibbled his way down her stomach.

He parted her legs and swiped at her clit with his tongue. A long sweep that had her sitting half upright.

He raised his gaze to hers before continuing, knowing that she could watch him as he licked her, slow teasing laps at her clit alternating with faster circles that had her hips moving beneath his mouth.

He anchored her hips with his hands and picked up the pace, gauging her reaction to his ministrations and varying the speed accordingly. Until he knew she was close and one lick would send her over the edge.

She came with the type of honesty he'd expect from Lucy: loud, proud, ecstatic.

He loved it. Loved her uninhibited response, loved her keenness for more when her legs fell open wider.

Eager to be inside her, he sheathed himself in record time and rejoined her on the bed, propped over her.

'That was fantastic,' she said, her eyes wide and passion-glazed.

'First of many,' he said, nudging her entrance, gritting his teeth against the urge to plunge inside her.

'All night, you said?' She wrapped her legs around his waist and he eased inside her, the exquisite pleasure of her tightness making his head spin. 'I like a man who can keep his promises.'

'Yep, all night long,' he managed to say, before instinct took over.

There were no more words, no more teasing. Just the two of them, caught up in the heat.

Their pants and groans mingled as their sweat-slicked bodies came together.

Hard. Soft.

Fast. Slow.

Lucy's blunt nails scraping his back.

Her fingers digging into his ass.

Urging him on.

Cash didn't need the encouragement. His body had taken on a life of its own, knowing on a visceral level how best to please Lucy.

Her thighs clamped his hips in a vice-like grip as he thrust into her over and over, the tension coiling through his body, the pressure building to exquisite agony.

'Jeez, Cash…oh…yeah…' Lucy yelled, her insides

squeezing him, spasm after spasm, mind-blowingly incredible.

His orgasm slammed into him a second after she screamed his name and the strength of it blanked his mind.

He had no idea how long it took him to refocus but when he did, he found Lucy grinning up at him as if he'd just conquered Everest.

In a way, he had. The years of emotional detachment he'd fostered where women were concerned had just been obliterated by sex with a woman who made him feel more than a physical release.

Because for the first time ever, Cash felt the uncharacteristic urge to cuddle and snuggle and cook a gigantic fried breakfast in the morning.

It scared the crap out of him.

'Be back in a minute,' he said, easing out of her and managing to stand on his unsurprisingly shaky legs as he padded to the bathroom.

But not before he'd glimpsed a flicker of regret in her expressive eyes, as if she was worried she'd disappointed him somehow.

Damn, he'd better get back in there and make it up to her the only way he knew how.

Orgasms. Straight up, and all night long, as promised.

CHAPTER NINE

LUCY'S EYELIDS CRANKED open at five a.m., her usual waking time. No matter what time she fell asleep, her body clock buzzed her awake when most sane people were still slumbering.

She snuggled under the covers for her regulatory five minutes, waiting for her head to clear enough so she could mentally list the day's jobs.

However, as the sleep fog cleared work wasn't the first thing that came to mind. Oh no, that honour belonged to a scorching memory of what she'd done with Cash. Many times over.

She flung a forearm over her eyes. Yeah, as if that would block out the memories.

A soft exhalation of breath, almost imperceptible, to her right made her stiffen.

And that was the moment she really woke up.

She hadn't left last night after they'd done those wickedly pleasurable things.

She was still in Cash's bed.

Dragging in a few calming breaths, she waited until his breathing resumed regularity before rolling her head towards him.

He had his back to her, rising and falling gently with

each breath he took. By the rhythm, he was still asleep. Thank goodness.

With her head a muddle and her body twinging in places it hadn't twinged in a long time, the last thing she needed was an awkward morning-after chat.

She knew how it would play out. Cash being glib and charming, her clutching a sheet as she made a dash to the bathroom, hoping to locate her clothes along the way.

Clothes that were downstairs if memory served her correctly.

What on earth had got into her last night?

She'd been bold and provocative, deliberately teasing him, strutting around in her underwear like a lingerie model. Pushing his buttons. Running up the stairs. Taunting him.

And the way she'd openly devoured him with her eyes when he'd stripped to nothing... Her cheeks heated at the thought.

Yeah, it would be much better if he continued to sleep and she slipped away to nurse her confusion in peace. Because that was exactly what she felt: utterly bamboozled.

Being intimate with Cash last night had made her feel emboldened and powerful and sexy.

Three things she'd never felt with Adrian. With her ex, she'd deferred to him in everything, including the bedroom.

But Cash was a very different man and he made her feel...feminine. Something she didn't get to feel too often with her hands stuck in dirt or mulch.

Cash seemed to see beneath her detached exterior and she responded by allowing her natural playfulness to come through.

It felt great. In fact, it felt downright amazing and

that more than anything made her want to flee before he tempted her into staying.

Because he would, no doubt about it. He'd roll over in bed, all sleepy and tousled, and reach for her. Wanting a repeat of last night, and the way she was feeling now she'd be all too willing to acquiesce.

No, she had to escape now.

With her gaze riveted to Cash's sleeping form for any signs of movement, she eased towards the side of the bed and slid out onto the floor sideways.

Cash didn't move and she breathed a sigh of relief. Relief short-lived when she glanced around and couldn't find her underwear.

Mentally cursing her wanton abandon last night, she crawled around the end of the bed, spying her bra and panties within reach.

She wriggled into her panties, refastened her bra and stood, casting a last longing look at the bed.

Cash slumbered on and, for one crazy second, she wanted to climb back into bed and kiss him awake.

The way he'd made her feel last night…exhilarated, wild, *alive*…multiple orgasms plus sensational sex, with a guy she could actually like.

If any of this was real.

That thought was enough to propel her feet towards the door.

Last night had been fabulous. But it had been a one-off. A few hours of unbridled pleasure between two people who had fostered an attraction by their play-acting.

The sooner they got back to faking it, the better.

'Lucy, Mrs Gramola at the deli said she saw you kissing some hunk online.' Gram slid another pancake onto Lucy's plate. 'I told her she was cuckoo.'

Uh-oh. The last thing Lucy needed after a sleepless night was to face one of Gram's legendary interrogations.

She didn't want to have to discuss Cash in any way, shape or form. Not after the best sex of her life. All night long, as he'd promised. She had a lot of respect for a man who kept his promises.

Lucy quickly shovelled a forkful of pancake into her mouth and tried not to choke.

'She is cuckoo, right?' Gram hovered over her, waving the spatula in the air.

Lucy chewed and mumbled a non-committal response.

Predictably, Gram wouldn't be deterred. She banged the pan back on the stove, ditched the spatula and sat opposite Lucy.

'What's going on, missie?'

'Nothing,' Lucy said, prevented from forking more pancake into her mouth when Gram laid a hand on her forearm.

'Would you prefer I head back down to the deli and hear the gossip from Mrs Gramola?'

Considering the Gramolas were known for their notorious gossip spreading with every sale of small goods, Lucy had no choice but to set Gram straight.

She laid her fork on her plate and nudged it away. 'You know I'm doing that mega landscaping job in Williamstown?'

Wariness pinched Gram's mouth. 'For that handsome man paying fifty grand for his new garden?'

Lucy nodded. 'Yeah. Well, Cash wanted something in return.'

Gram's eyes narrowed with suspicion. 'To attend a few functions, right?'

'Um…yeah.' There was no way Lucy could sugar-coat this so she blurted it all in one go. 'And to pose as his girlfriend for a week in a PR stunt leading up to Valentine's Day.'

Gram's mouth dropped open.

'I know, sounds crazy, huh? But there's not much to it, really. We attend a few functions, the couples are filmed and snippets posted on the PR firm's website for people to vote.'

'Vote for what? The most delusional, exhibitionist pair of losers?'

Lucy chuckled, buoyed by Gram's signature bluntness.

'Honestly, Gram? I feel the same way. But it seemed a small price to pay to save your house.'

Gram sighed and shook her head. 'I should never have agreed to accept that money from you.'

Lucy patted her hand. 'I wanted to do it.'

'But to parade around on the Internet...kissing some stranger?'

'Cash isn't a stranger.'

Not any more. Not after last night. She now knew his body in intimate detail: where he liked to be licked... stroked...nibbled...the ticklish spot near his armpits, the zigzag birth mark on his left hip pointing to his sizable...assets.

Gram tilted her head to one side, studying her. 'Well, well, well. Never thought I'd see the day.'

Lucy ducked her head and stared at her pancake drowning in maple syrup. 'What?'

'You're blushing.' Gram sniggered. 'And you've got a glow I haven't seen since...' She trailed off and cleared her throat. 'Never mind that. I've seen his pic that first time you showed me online. Now tell me more about this young man you've been kissing in public.' Gram winked. 'And don't spare the details.'

Lucy didn't want to talk about Cash kissing her. Because then she might be tempted to relive in exquisite detail every kiss last night...every caress...every touch.

'Cash is a good guy. We get on okay—'

'I want to see him.'

No way. She knew Gram. Inflicting her on Cash would result in a catastrophic attempt at matchmaking or interrogating or both.

'He's a busy guy. I don't think—'

'I meant see him online, with you,' Gram said, exasperation audible.

'Oh, right,' Lucy said, not knowing what was worse. Launching Gram on Cash in person or showing Gram their X-rated pash at the disco.

'I'm not getting any younger, dear.' Gram drummed her fingers on the table with exaggerated impatience.

Without any other excuses to dredge up, Lucy fired up her electronic tablet, clicked on her bookmarks and opened up the PR firm's website.

She'd already watched the footage countless times, and had moved on from cringing to being transfixed in voyeuristic heaven.

They looked like a real couple on that dance floor. A couple that couldn't keep their hands off each other. A couple in love.

Didn't surprise her they'd ranked the highest after that little impromptu make-out session. Pervy people loved that sort of thing. Problem was, she did too. Loved Cash kissing her as if there were no tomorrow, that was.

Heat flushed her cheeks just thinking about the very inventive ways he'd kissed her last night.

'Whoever can make you look like that, my dear? I have to see this kiss.' Gram pointed to her cheeks and mock fanned them.

'Here. Knock yourself out.' She thrust the tablet at Gram and inadvertently braced.

Gram was a pretty good judge of character. She'd called Adrian a sleazy, heartbreaking upstart after the first time she'd met him. Turned out, Gram had been spot on. Which made Lucy all the sadder that Pops had fooled her for so many years.

Gram hit play on the video clip and settled back in her chair to watch while Lucy took the opportunity to finish her pancakes. A girl couldn't face an impending interrogation on an empty stomach.

'Oh my Lordy…' Gram stared at the tablet, her wide eyes almost a perfect match for her O-shaped mouth. 'You've got a live one there, my girl.'

And didn't Lucy know it.

She'd been so smug at the start of this week, thinking she had the upper hand by almost doubling her fee for the job in exchange for a little harmless acting.

She'd expected to breeze through the functions with an updated wardrobe, a new haircut and a few simpering smiles.

She hadn't expected Cash Burgess to be so darn appealing, with deeper facets to his personality than she'd ever imagined.

Like his ability to trust her, and gain her trust, enough for them to exchange details of their painful pasts. Throw in his charm twenty-four-seven and a body that would tempt a nun, and she'd never stood a chance.

When the clip finished, Gram laid the tablet carefully on the table and stared at Lucy with a mix of awe and glee.

'You said you're pretending to be his girlfriend?'

Lucy nodded.

Gram beamed as if she'd just won the lottery. 'Luce,

I love you, but you're stark raving bonkers if you think for one second there's anything remotely fake about the two of you being together.'

Lucy's heart sank. She'd been afraid of this. Gram latching onto her very temporary romance with Cash and turning it into a grand passion.

'Gram, we're attracted, and it's been a while since I've dated, so that kiss kinda happened out of the blue—'

'When do I get to meet him?'

'Gram...' Lucy shook her head. 'This thing with Cash isn't real—'

'Bollocks.' Gram leaned forward and grasped her chin, ensuring she couldn't look away. 'I knew this man must be special the moment you walked in here this morning. You're radiant.' Gram paused, as if weighing her next words carefully. 'I've never seen you look like this. Ever.'

Gram's polite way of saying that included Adrian.

But Gram was wrong. She had *loved* Adrian, had been smitten by him. Her feelings for Cash weren't remotely close to...

Feelings?

Oh no. No, no, no. Lucy didn't have feelings for Cash. She couldn't. It wasn't part of her plan to fake it.

Gram released her chin and folded her arms, her expression smug. 'And you say you're doing this man's garden even after this week is up?' Gram winked. 'Clever girl.'

Then why did Lucy feel incredibly dumb?

Agreeing to Cash's scheme in the first place might have seemed a good idea at the time but now? Working for him would've been okay, if she hadn't slept with the guy.

So much for Valentine's Day putting an end to her misery.

After what they'd done last night? Looked as if the festivities were just getting started.

Because of the time he was investing in the PR functions, Cash had scheduled back-to-back work meetings all day.

Which would've been okay, if he'd managed to get more than an hour's sleep last night.

Not that he was complaining. What had kept him busy into the small hours had blown his mind.

His only regret after a sensational night was that she'd crept out before five-thirty a.m.—and he'd let her.

He should've stopped her, should've said something. Instead, he'd taken the coward's way out, feigning sleep as she slipped on her underwear and did the walk of shame from his bedroom.

That had been half his problem: not knowing what to say. If he'd said thanks, he would've sounded like a schmuck. If he'd asked what she was doing today, ditto.

The truth was, he'd wanted to say all that and more. But the words wouldn't come and by the time he'd made up his mind to speak up, she'd gone.

He could've called her, but he'd been tied up all day and had just finished his last meeting of the day, at nine p.m.

Thankfully, his plan was working, and the positive feedback from the Valentine's Day competition had ensured several clients in danger of walking had re-signed. In fact, it was all his clients wanted to talk about, before getting down to discussing money business. He accepted their ribbing with grace and played up the hokey romance angle.

But when clients asked about Lucy, he artfully dodged the questions and steered the conversation onto safer ground. Namely, away from the woman he was in danger of falling for.

Ludicrous, for a guy who would never entertain the thought of a relationship that lasted past a few dates, let alone a full-blown commitment.

Yet the time he'd spent with Lucy, both in and out of the bedroom, had him contemplating what could be, given half a chance.

And that thought alone was enough to have him grabbing his mobile phone to send her a message.

He needed to establish distance. Something he should've done first thing this morning when he'd found himself mooning around the office.

Cash didn't do relationships and, despite outlining last night that they'd have sex without strings attached, looked as if his heart hadn't got the memo.

Lucy had had no problem leaving this morning without looking back. And she certainly hadn't picked up the phone to see how his day had been after what they'd shared.

So this terse message he had to send to re-establish equilibrium? It was for his benefit.

His thumb tapped on the screen.

2 busy to catch up before skate date.
Will C U there

Brief to the point of rudeness. Cash hesitated a second before hitting send.

He wanted to establish that nothing had changed post-sex. Prove to himself that the potent memories of intimacy plaguing him were nothing more than sleep deprivation.

But when he found himself staring at the phone, willing Lucy to respond, he knew it would take more than a pithy message to re-establish some much-needed distance between them.

Her succinct 'OK' reply should've made him happy. It didn't. Once again, he was back to thinking about Lucy: what she was doing, how did she feel about last night, whether she'd be up for a repeat.

Cursing his obsession, he flung himself into his office chair, unwittingly drawn to the computer screen. He shouldn't watch that clip of them at the disco again, he really shouldn't, but after a hellish day with little sleep he allowed himself the indulgence.

He hit play, clasped his hands behind his head and leaned back, glued to the passion unfolding on the screen.

Cash never lost his head. He weighed up every decision, usually with dollar signs in his eyes. Yet staring at the way he'd steamed up the screen with Lucy, he'd moved way past losing his head and landed straight in uncharted territory.

God, Lucy was hot. She had no artifice, her genuine responses a major turn-on. Something she'd demonstrated last night in the privacy of his bedroom; and how.

If he had any sense, he'd pick up the phone right now and call her.

And say what? *Sorry for the a-hole text. Come over. I'm lonely. I miss you?*

With an angry growl he sat forward and hit the escape key, the screen instantly reverting to a saver.

Yeah, as if that would get Lucy out of his mind.

Ideally, their tryst should end on Valentine's Day, but with her making over his garden she'd be here daily for weeks...wearing those tight shorts and tank tops...exposing tempting expanses of tanned skin...skin he'd tasted...

He cursed again and strode towards the door.

One more function to get through tomorrow—roller-skating—then the ball, and he was home free.

Objective achieved. Reputation intact. Business booming. Money rolling in.

He should be ecstatic.

So why the annoying niggle that he'd be missing out on something once this week ended?

CHAPTER TEN

'SORRY I DIDN'T call yesterday, got caught up in meetings all day 'til late.' Cash hated how trite his apology sounded, when in reality he'd been unsure of his reception and her reaction following their night together.

So he'd sent her an impersonal text instead to push her away. Nice.

'Not a problem.' She glanced up from lacing up her skate. 'I had a busy day too.'

Cash knew he had to broach what had happened between them but, for the first time in his life, he was clueless and inarticulate.

She finished lacing up and stood, her teasing smile indication she had a zinger incoming. 'Though have to admit, I thought you were being a wuss and avoiding me.'

'Why?'

'Post-coital embarrassment?' She threw it out there, casual as you like, another classic example of her signature bluntness.

'From what I recall, nothing to be embarrassed about,' he said, lowering his head to whisper in her ear. 'Unless the many times you screamed my name made you feel uncomfortable—'

'Shh!' She shoved him away but the dreamy look in

her eyes spoke volumes. 'What happened in the bedroom stays in the bedroom.'

'That doesn't include you stripping downstairs. Or that feisty little sprint up the stairs—'

'If you're trying to make me break my leg, you're going about it the right way,' she said, her frown as fake as the pout.

Because, like him, she was reliving those moments he'd just mentioned: the flirting, the sizzle, the passion.

They'd been incredible together and merely thinking about it made him hard.

So much for re-establishing distance.

'Stop trying to distract me with...' She trailed off, a faint pink staining her cheeks, and he laughed.

'With scorching memories of how we burned up the sheets?'

'Something like that,' she muttered, casting him a coy glance from beneath her lashes. 'Though have to admit, I'm surprised you're talking about it.'

'Why?'

He'd talk about their sexy interlude all day long if it made her look flushed and flustered and incredibly cute. With the added bonus of focusing on the physical between them, keeping it light made him feel better about the idiotic way he was floundering out of his depth and contemplating more than sex.

She glanced around and, satisfied there was no one within listening distance, slid a little closer to him. 'Because we know that night was an aberration. We'd both divulged too much at the picnic and mistook it for closeness.' She shrugged. 'Throw in the natural attraction between us, wasn't any great surprise we ended up in bed.'

Everything Lucy said made sense but it didn't mean Cash had to like it. From the moment she'd dismissed their sensational night together as an *aberration*, he'd wanted to protest. Wanted to tell her he'd never had a night like it. Wanted to say that he liked her, beyond the sex.

But he didn't say any of those things, because Lucy had just given him the perfect out. What he'd wanted since last night.

She didn't want to complicate what they had with emotions and he respected her for that. She didn't expect their night of sex to equal a relationship. She didn't want anything from him beyond the money.

He should be ecstatic. She'd articulated brilliantly what he'd been trying to achieve with that god-awful text. So why the burning disappointment?

'Glad we're on the same page,' he said, feeling like a heel as he snagged her hand. Because despite how she'd brushed off their encounter, and how much he wanted to agree with her, dismissing their connection that night felt plain wrong.

'Are these people for real?' Eager to steer the conversation onto safer ground, Cash held Lucy's hand tight as they waited their turn to enter the roller-skating rink. 'Who does this once they're past the age of ten?'

Lucy laughed, the joyful sound making something in his chest twang. 'I used to love skating when I was a kid.'

'Not me.'

He'd been too busy doing his homework or tidying up the two-bedroom flat he'd shared with his dad to have time to indulge in frivolous activities.

'But you can skate, right?' She shot him a concerned look and he decided to have a little fun.

He bit his bottom lip to keep from laughing and shook his head. 'Not very well.'

Her concern morphed to panic. 'You're not going to fall and drag me down with you?'

'Maybe I need you to hold my hand real tight and not let go?' Any excuse.

A tiny crease appeared between her brows. 'You should hold onto the rail along the outskirts of the rink. I think that's safest.'

'For who?'

'Everybody.'

He ducked down to whisper in her ear, throwing in a little stumble for good measure, and her arm instantly shot out to steady him. 'You should give me a kiss for good luck.'

She eased away to glare. 'I'm not falling for that—'

He kissed her anyway, a soft tender melding of lips that quickly escalated into heat and yearning.

He'd thought having sex with Lucy would get her out of his system, would assuage what he assumed was a raging case of lust because she was so different from the women he usually hung out with.

It hadn't. If anything, he wanted her even more now. And damned if he could figure out how to extract himself gracefully from this unfamiliar scenario.

'You're up, folks.' An attendant interrupted them and not a moment too soon, considering he wouldn't be able to skate at all if he was physically impeded below the belt.

He expected Lucy to look annoyed at yet another public display of affection. Instead, her goofy grin as she entwined her fingers through his told him she liked hanging out together as much as he did.

'Was that one for the cameras?' she said, pointing to them on the sidelines.

He shook his head. 'That one was for me.'

He hauled her against him and planted another hot quickie against her lips. 'That one's for you.'

She cupped his cheek with her free hand and stared at him with a seriousness that scared the crap out of him.

'I think all this fake relationship stuff is starting to get to us.'

He nodded. 'It's starting to feel pretty real to me.'

Cash unwittingly held his breath, waiting for Lucy to say something, anything, to reinforce what he already knew: they were halfway to being crazy about each other.

'Move it along, people.' The attendant all but shoved them onto the rink, shattering the moment.

Cash should've been glad. Last thing he needed was for Lucy to articulate she'd developed feelings for him. So why did he feel incredibly let down?

She nudged him towards the railing. 'Hold on there and watch an expert strut her stuff.'

He managed a meek nod. 'Okay.'

He watched Lucy shoot out into the crowd, weaving her way through the skaters with poise and speed. She didn't hesitate once, darting and weaving like a pro. She was magnificent. And damned if his chest didn't give another betraying twang.

He waited until she hit the final turn and made eye contact, before he pushed off the railing, picked up speed and executed a perfect backward-double turn.

Lucy gaped as he grinned and shot her a jaunty half-salute.

Who's the expert now? He wanted to yell across the rink. Childish? Absolutely, but he loved teasing her. Loved making her eyes sparkle and her lips part a smidgeon before she smiled.

He skated in slow half-circles on the spot, waiting for her to catch up.

Snapping out of her shocked trance after his little display, she sped up, racing towards him.

She didn't see one of the other couples skate a tad too close.

She didn't anticipate the girl's skate snagging on her guy's.

She didn't have time to avoid the couple that sprawled at her feet.

Cash saw it all as if in slow motion. Powerless, he watched the woman he cared about trip and land hard.

He swore and raced across the rink. A crowd had gathered by the time he reached her side and he knelt, unable to breathe, pain ricocheting through his chest.

'Luce, are you okay?'

She groaned in response and pushed herself up into a half-sitting position.

'Don't move. I'll call an ambulance.'

She shot him a death glare. 'I don't need an ambulance, you dufus, but you might by the time I've finished with you.'

His sheepish smile didn't help matters. 'You were so cocky and condescending, I wanted to take you down a peg or two.'

'You succeeded.' She winced as she tried to straighten her legs. 'Now help me up.'

'Show's over, folks,' he said, dispersing the crowd by waving them away before sliding his hands under Lucy's armpits and helping her stand.

He heard her muttered curses and bit back a smile. She'd be sore and bruised for a while, and he'd like nothing better than to massage her pain away.

'Make sure you kill each and every one of those bloody cameramen before my fall ends up on the website,' she said, taking his arm when he offered it.

'Anything for you, sweetheart.'

The moment the tongue-in-cheek response fell from his lips, Cash knew it was true.

He'd do anything for this strong, capable, amazing woman.

Those few seconds when she'd gone down and he couldn't stop it? They might just have been the worst of his life. He'd do anything to protect her. Which meant...

Hell, he liked her. Really liked her.

Crap.

This was so not in his plans.

He needed to get back on familiar territory, to keep things light-hearted between them. It was the only way.

He helped her off the rink, eased her onto a seat and knelt at her feet, loosening her laces. 'There's an upside to your humiliation.'

Not amused by his try at levity, she frowned. 'Really?'

'Yeah.' He eased off her first skate. 'Just think of all the sore bits I get to kiss better.'

Her glower immediately softened. 'But I'm sore all over.'

'Now you're talking.' He winked and eased off the other skate. 'Want to cut this session short, head back to my place and make out?'

She rolled her eyes, but not before he'd seen a spark of excitement. 'Just because we're at a skate rink doesn't mean you need to resort to teen vocab. Make out? Seriously?'

'I'm deadly serious.' He stood and scooped her into his arms to prove it.

'Put me down,' she said, a half-hearted protest tempered by her silly grin. 'You're still wearing skates. We'll both go down.'

'That's what I'm hoping,' he murmured, seeing the

exact moment she cottoned onto his innuendo when her cheeks flushed crimson.

She glanced away, unable to meet his eyes. 'The faster you put me down, the faster we can get our shoes on and leave.'

'Eager to get me alone?' He lowered her back to the chair and sat next to her, undoing his skates in record time.

'Eager for a long, hot soak in some Epsom salts more like it,' she muttered, grimacing as she raised an arm to run a hand through her hair.

'Be back in a sec.' He grabbed their shoes in record time, eager to sink into that hot bath right alongside her.

Kneeling at her feet, he held out her shoe and took her foot in the other. 'These yours, Cinders?'

'You're no Prince Charming,' she said, tempering her comeback with a coy smile as he carefully slid her shoes onto her feet.

'I'd like to be.'

He meant it too. He'd like to sweep this wonderful woman off her feet, because he had a feeling she wasn't used to the attention.

Didn't take a genius to figure out she'd been burned badly by her bastard ex cheating on her. And for her to marry, she must've loved the guy very much. Which was interesting, because Lucy didn't seem the impulsive type, so how long had she dated the ex? Who was he? A family friend? Love at first sight?

For the first time ever he actually found himself caring about a girlfriend's past.

As to his feelings for Lucy, he had his answer right there. Using the girlfriend label with a woman wasn't in his DNA. He dated women. He had female acquaintances. He had female friends with benefits.

But he didn't have girlfriends. Girlfriends conjured up visions of lust fading to dislike, irrational demands and a badgering for lifelong commitment. Only to have the whole thing fall apart when one or the other in the partnership got tired of the other.

He'd seen it firsthand with his parents; and the resultant fallout. It hadn't been pretty. In fact, it had scarred his dad for life and he never wanted to depend on another human being for his happiness. Ever.

So where did that leave his relationship with Lucy?

He cared too much about her to revert to being acquaintances once this week was over. But he didn't want to care too much for fear of stuffing up everything.

'You want to be my Prince Charming?' She made it sound as if he'd offered to push her out of a plane without a parachute. 'Good one.'

She winked, as if he'd made a gaff.

And the fact she hadn't taken him seriously hurt more than it should.

So Cash did the only thing possible. Shirked the hard stuff for now, until he could get his head around all the new feelings ricocheting around inside him.

'If you've finished laughing at your rescuer, I'll get you home.' He swept her into his arms before she could protest, and, to his surprise, she meekly wrapped her arms around his neck and snuggled in for the ride.

'Thanks,' she murmured somewhere in the vicinity of his chest as she rested her cheek against it.

As he carried her out of the skate rink to the applause of onlookers, he kinda liked having her dependent on him.

Lucy should've been uncomfortable with Cash perched on the edge of the bathtub, filling up her wine glass. But she wasn't. And that spoke volumes on how she viewed this relationship.

Because it was a relationship.

However they liked to dress it up, pretend it was fake for the PR, whatever, Lucy knew without a doubt that they'd moved into relationship territory.

Cash's expression after she'd fallen at the rink hadn't been that of a disengaged guy faking it for the cameras. And for a terrifying second, as he'd skated towards her at breakneck speed, she'd wanted to blurt exactly how she was feeling.

Like an A-grade ass, she'd fallen for her fake boy-friend.

Worse, it didn't terrify her as it should.

Having him pick her up, look after her, bring her back to her place and draw a bath made her feel good. Maybe being dependent on someone wasn't so scary if it was the right person.

'I'm hoping the warmth and the glass of Shiraz you've consumed has lulled you enough that I can ask you some-thing.' He placed the bottle on the bathroom cabinet and folded his arms. 'Have you dated much since your mar-riage?'

The question came from left field and Lucy would've usually told him to shove it or given a flippant answer. But caring about someone meant letting down her guard. And it had been a long time since she'd done that.

'No. Dating hasn't been high on my list of priorities since I divorced Adrian.'

He glowered as she said her ex's name, as if he wanted to pummel the guy. She knew the feeling.

'Why not? You're young, you're gorgeous, you must've had a stack of offers.'

She loved how free he was with compliments, even

though he was slightly delusional if he thought she was gorgeous. 'None of the offers interested me.'

'And now?'

She had no idea what he was asking so she took a sip of wine, another, buying time to formulate an answer that wouldn't get her into trouble.

He placed a hand on her shoulder. 'It's a simple enough question, Luce. Because I think we've moved past our original agreement and entered murky territory.'

She admired his honesty. But could he handle her bluntness?

'You want me to spell it out? Fine.' The bubbles shifted as she eased onto her side to face him. 'You're nothing like what I expected. I like you. But we're from different worlds and I'm not sure I'm ready to take a chance on a guy like you.'

He frowned. 'A guy like me?'

She dragged in a breath and blew it out. 'You're wealthy, successful and a permanent feature in Melbourne's social scene.'

He opened his mouth to respond and she held up a water-pruned finger. 'You're also like my ex.'

He reacted as if she'd called his manhood into question, shooting to his feet to tower over her. 'I'd never cheat on you.'

She hated doing this, but if she didn't articulate her concerns now, there'd be no going forward for them. 'Maybe not. But Adrian was smitten with me at the start too. He liked our differences. But apparently he got tired of them after a while and that's why he started looking elsewhere. So pardon me for being a cynic.'

Cash stared at her as if she'd sprouted horns. 'You're kidding, right? You bought that douchebag's excuses, blaming you?' His fingers curled into fists. 'I'm nothing like him and I would've hoped you'd have figured that out by now.'

She shrugged and held out her hands, palm up. 'I'm just telling you how it is. So there can be no misinterpretations later.'

His hands relaxed as he shot her a dubious glance. 'There's going to be a later?'

'If you're lucky.'

She sank back into the bubbles and closed her eyes, needing to blot out the sight of a righteous, indignant Cash ready to slay dragons for her, before she blubbered.

Because that strange burning in her eyes definitely signalled the onset of tears and she didn't want to cry in front of him. She'd answered enough questions for one day. No way did she want him asking more.

For if she did cry it wouldn't be tears of sadness. For the first time in a long time Lucy was happy.

She had a guy sensitive enough to ask questions and to respect her answers. A guy willing to protect her. A guy who cared.

Lucy squeezed her eyes tight to prevent the slightest tear seepage. Until she heard a slight splash, the water lapped higher on her chest and a foot brushed her outer thigh.

Her eyes snapped open to see Cash settling into the bath, his arms draped on the side of the tub, his grin smug.

'There isn't room in here for two.'

He winked. 'Exactly.'

Those aches and pains sustained from the skating fall? Faded into oblivion as Cash demonstrated exactly how a bathtub built for one could accommodate two.

CHAPTER ELEVEN

THE NEXT MORNING, Cash postponed a seminar to go see the one person who could get him out of his funk.

His dad. They might not have got on so well as Cash was growing up, but they'd been all each other had for too long not to know each other inside out. If his old man couldn't help with Cash's problems, no one could.

'What brings you by?' Ronnie Burgess sat on his small balcony, sipping black tea, his daily ritual since he'd retired from his job at the local car parts factory a few years ago.

'Do I need an excuse to visit my dad?' Cash squeezed onto a too-small wrought-iron chair next to his dad and looked out over the backstreets of Collingwood.

They'd moved into this flat after Mum threw them out and, despite Cash offering to relocate his dad, buy him a house/apartment/whatever he wanted, Ronnie refused. Cash had no idea if it was stubborn pride preventing his dad from accepting his offer, or a determination to remind himself never to repeat the mistakes of the past, but Ronnie was firmly entrenched in this working-class suburb.

'No excuse needed, you know that.' Ronnie sipped at his tea and studied Cash. 'But it looks like you've got something on your mind, son.'

'Why do you say that?'

'Because you look like you haven't slept in a week.'

Wasn't that the truth. Ever since Lucy had agreed to his crazy scheme, he'd been running on empty. Vacillating between throwing himself into work to forget about her and spending as much time with her as possible because he couldn't forget her.

'Got a lot on my mind,' Cash said, pouring himself a cuppa. 'Need a little down time.'

'I never would have thought I'd be the one to say this, but you work too hard.' Ronnie continued to study him with an intensity that made Cash uncomfortable. 'Not such a bad thing though, considering the success you've made of yourself.'

'Thanks.' Cash stirred sugar into his tea, unsure how to broach a subject guaranteed to put his dad in a mood.

'You should ease back a bit though. Take time to smell the gardenias...' Ronnie trailed off, his expression stricken, before he shook his head. 'Jeez, that was your mum's favourite flower. The last time I said that was to her.'

'You never mentioned her when I was growing up.'

Sorrow clouded Ronnie's eyes. 'What's there to mention? She was the love of my life. Despite our differences I thought we could make things work. I was a fool.'

Not exactly the pep talk Cash needed to hear, but he was glad his dad was finally discussing his mum.

'I saw her once.' Cash added a splash of milk to his tea and stirred. 'She got me into a theatre opening but disappeared before I could thank her.'

Ronnie sipped at his tea, his hand visibly shaking. 'You've never felt the urge to contact her?'

'Not really.' At last, the opportunity to broach the subject he'd long wondered about. 'Why'd she do it, Dad? Throw us out?'

And never contact her only child?

Because that was at the crux of many burning questions when it came to his mother. How the hell could she discard her child like yesterday's garbage?

'Honestly?' Ronnie pinched the bridge of his nose, closed his eyes, before opening them slowly. 'I don't know. Your mother was like a butterfly, always flitting from thing to thing. I reckon I was one of those things she stuck to for longer than most for her, before she moved on again.'

Ronnie tapped his temple. 'There were times I wondered if she had a problem up here. Undiagnosed.' He sighed. 'Her flightiness worsened after she had you...

'She had a fear of settling in one spot for too long, which is why she never agreed to any of my marriage proposals.' Ronnie topped up his cup from the chipped porcelain pot. 'I was never under any illusions when it came to your mum. I was her walk on the wild side. She probably only shacked up with me to piss off her snooty parents. And when she tired of me, she moved on.'

Cash should've felt better he'd learned a little more about his mum's rationale. Instead, he couldn't fathom how such a heartless woman had stood still long enough to have a child.

'It was never about you.' For the first time in years, his dad touched him, laying a hand on his forearm for a second before removing it. 'She just never had the capacity to love anything for longer than five minutes.'

A chill crept across the back of Cash's neck as the implication sank in.

Was he the same as his mum?

He'd never grown attached to anyone, had never been

in a committed relationship. Until now, he'd always used excuses like his business or not being hurt like his dad and ending up bitter and twisted for not willing to commit.

But what if it went deeper than that? What if his DNA programmed him to be as flaky as his mum?

'Have you met someone?' Ronnie eyeballed him from over the rim of his teacup. 'Is that what has you in a state?'

Cash nodded. 'She's pretty incredible but I'm not really sure I want to get involved.'

'More than you are already?' Ronnie chuckled. 'Son, let me give you a tip. When a man looks as blindsided as you do, it's too late to contemplate getting *involved*.'

Ronnie made a chopping gesture at his neck. 'You're in it up to here already.'

Cash managed a wry grin. 'For a confirmed bachelor, you're pretty wise.'

His dad's amusement faded, replaced by a sombreness that darkened his eyes. 'Don't make the same mistake I did, son. I let my bitterness taint everything, including my relationship with you. I let a bruised ego and wounded pride stop me from engaging with anyone, even my own son.' He shook his head. 'You deserve better than that and if you've met a special woman, take a chance on creating something good together.'

Was it as simple as that?

Take a chance on Lucy?

He didn't want to create something good with her. He wanted to create something great.

'Thanks, Dad.' Cash slapped Ronnie on the back. 'For an old codger you're pretty damn wise.'

'Pity it took me so many years to wise up.' Ronnie raised his teacup in a cheers salute. 'Good luck to you, son. If you're smitten with a woman, you're going to need it.'

Cash couldn't agree more.

For the first time in years, Lucy took the day off.

Cash left at seven after serving her breakfast in bed and that was where she remained, rescheduling her day's jobs via a few phone calls.

She burrowed down in the blankets and spent a leisurely hour watching a mindless soap opera before dragging her sore body into the shower.

Considering the fall she'd had, it could've been worse. But the bruises on her body weren't what kept her home today.

She needed a mental health day.

Because her mental health wasn't so crash hot at the moment.

Some time in the middle of the night, with Cash holding her gently in his arms, she accepted the truth.

She loved him.

A realisation that ensured insomnia for the rest of the night. Not such a bad thing at the time, as she watched him sleep, her infatuation fuelling her illicit vigil: the way his lashes cast shadows on his cheeks, the way his mouth relaxed into a semi-smile, the way his lips pursed as he puffed out tiny snores.

Yeah, she had it bad. And for the first time in for ever she didn't care.

It was time to take a chance on love again. And she couldn't have fallen for a better man.

Cradling her third coffee of the day, she eased into the wicker chair on her back veranda, content to do nothing but scan her pristine garden.

It had been the first thing she tackled when she moved

in, transforming the nondescript patch of grass into a Japanese garden. She loved the tranquillity, had needed a haven at the time, and had spent many loving hours designing the placement of alternating squares of slate and white pebbles, the hip-height lantern, the bonsai.

She'd done a lot of thinking in this garden, had cried many tears and eventually let go of her resentment towards Adrian. She hadn't forgotten or forgiven, but she'd made peace with herself: there was nothing she could've done in her marriage to change the outcome.

But she'd be lying to herself if she didn't acknowledge the lasting legacy that her failed marriage had left: a bone-deep insecurity that, no matter what she did or how she looked, she'd never be good enough.

She'd cradled those insecurities close to her chest, had used them as a protective mechanism for as long as she could remember. So what was it about Cash that allayed her deep-set fears and made her want to take a chance on love again?

'Thought I might find you here,' Gram said, strolling around the corner, a tube of liniment in one hand, and a cake container in the other.

'Hey, Gram,' Lucy said, patting the love seat next to her. 'What's in the box?'

'Your favourite peppermint choc cookies.' Gram sat, pried open the container and offered it to her. 'Looked like you'd need it.'

Confused, Lucy grabbed two cookies. 'What do you mean?'

Gram handed over the liniment tube. 'I saw your fall.'

'How…Gram, you're watching us on that stupid website?'

'And casting my vote.' Gram grinned and crammed a cookie into her mouth.

'I'm sure there must be a rule about relatives voting.'

Gram dabbed at the corners of her mouth for residual crumbs. 'Who cares? You're winning by a landslide so removing my vote won't make much difference.'

'We're winning?' Oddly enough, Lucy hadn't checked the website since they posted her disco pash with Cash. She'd been too busy falling for the guy to worry about little incidentals like people watching her fake relationship turn real.

Gram nodded. 'Not surprising, considering the way you two steam up the screen.'

'We don't—'

'You're in love with him.' Gram's eyes misted over. 'Not that I blame you. The way he took care of you after your fall? Carrying you in his arms? Whispering in your ear?'

Gram fanned her face. 'There's some serious romance going on between you two, my girl, and it's about time.'

Was it that obvious? Did the whole of Melbourne know she was head over heels for Cash Burgess?

'You deserve the best.' Gram tapped her bottom lip, pondering. 'I think this one's a keeper.'

'Like Pops?'

Some of the sparkle in Gram's eyes faded. 'I loved your grandfather dearly, but the way he deceived me?' She shook her head. 'We forgive the ones we love, sometimes to our detriment.'

Uh-oh, Lucy hadn't meant to open an old wound, but the way Gram said it sounded as if she'd known about Pops' addiction while he'd been alive...

'Did you know about his gambling?'

It was a possibility Lucy had never considered and it shocked her, the fact Gram might've tolerated such selfish behaviour from Pops. Behaviour that ultimately put Gram at risk of losing everything.

Shame twisted Gram's mouth. 'I had my suspicions after your grandfather retired. The long absences. The defensiveness when I asked for change from the grocery shopping. The mood swings after he returned from a day with his mates at the races.'

Gram snorted. 'At first I thought he might be having an affair so I asked him. He denied it.'

'And you believed him.'

Gram nodded. 'Our love was strong.'

Strong enough for Gram to defend him even now, after the heartache he'd put her through.

'I admired you, you know, when you had the guts to leave that scumbag Adrian,' Gram said, approval making her eyes gleam. 'You had the guts to confront the problem head-on.'

Lucy only just caught Gram's murmured, 'I wish I had.'

'We do what we have to do, and what feels right for us,' Lucy said, dusting cookie crumbs off her fingers. 'Your relationship with Pops was rock solid. I never had that with Adrian.'

Gram frowned. 'What do you mean?'

'It took me a long while to realise I was so smitten with Adrian at the start, and the lifestyle he provided, that I was living in a fantasy world.' Lucy sighed, wishing she'd wised up before she'd married the jerk. 'Our relationship was superficial. Adrian liked acquiring things and when he tired of playing with me, he played elsewhere.'

Gram patted her hand. 'I hated him, you know. Too smarmy.'

'So you said, but you should've rammed the message home.'

Gram shook her head. 'You were gloriously happy and I didn't want to ruin that for you.'

Lucy slipped an arm around Gram's waist and hugged. 'I guess we live and learn from our mistakes.'

Gram hugged her back. 'Is that why you stopped wearing fancy clothes and make-up? Because you thought that frippery was part of your fantasy world with *him*?'

Gram made *him* sound like something nasty she'd stepped in.

Lucy nodded. 'I guess I felt like I didn't need to keep up appearances any more, because if that Lucy wasn't good enough for Adrian, what was the point?'

'Not good enough? Luce, you were *too* good for that cretin.' Gram grabbed another cookie. 'He's nothing like your dashing young man now.'

No, Cash was nothing like Adrian, despite their similarities in the front they presented to the world: wealthy, polished, successful.

And she had every intention of telling him after the ball tomorrow night.

Their week would be up. But she didn't want it to end.

'I think I'm in love with him, Gram.' Lucy pressed her hands to her cheeks, willing the heat to subside whenever she thought about Cash and how he made her feel. 'How is that possible, in less than seven days?'

'We don't choose who we fall in love with.' Gram winked. 'I'm guessing his garden isn't the only thing you'll be working on.'

'Gram!' Lucy feigned shock, when in fact she was enjoying their chat. Enjoying being able to share her feelings with someone.

Because articulating her feelings for Cash made them

seem more real and less fanciful. After protecting her heart for so many years, she'd fallen for a guy in less than a week. It should be unfathomable, and crazy. Instead, being with Cash felt right.

She couldn't wait to see where they went from here.

'So what are you wearing to the ball?'

Lucy stood and took Gram's hand. 'Bring those cookies inside and I'll show you.'

Gram didn't need to be asked twice.

As they entered the house Lucy's mobile rang and one glance at the caller ID on the screen had her blushing.

'Gram, I have to take this.'

With a knowing smile, Gram nodded. 'I'll be in the bedroom waiting for you to show me this killer ball gown.'

Lucy smiled her thanks and stabbed at the answer button on the phone. 'Hey, you.'

'You could sound a little more enthusiastic to hear from me,' Cash said, his deep voice sending a thrill through her.

'I'm doing chest-high cheerleader kicks on the inside.'

He laughed. 'So how are you feeling? Still bruised and battered?'

'Much better after that bath last night...' She didn't need to say any more and, by his sharp intake of breath, Cash was remembering exactly how he'd soothed her sore muscles last night.

He'd stroked and caressed. Kneaded and massaged. Until she'd almost purred. She'd forgotten the humiliation of her spectacular fall being filmed and shown to thousands. She'd forgotten the complications of falling for a guy potentially wrong for her in every way. She'd forgotten everything bar how he made her feel.

As if she was the most cherished woman in the world.

'Minx.' He paused and cleared his throat. 'If you like, I can cut out of work for an hour, come over and repeat my extra-special massage technique just for you.'

Her body tingled all over at the thought. 'My gram's here.'

'Oo-kay then, rain check.'

She chuckled. 'Absolutely.'

'Though it'll have to be after the ball because I've got some stupid client function I have to attend tonight.'

'That's fine,' Lucy said, but deep down she knew it wasn't.

Why didn't he invite her along? Was it because his clients were gorgeous, glamorous starlets and he didn't think she belonged in that world?

It was one of the key differences between them that bothered her. His world was glitz and caviar and premieres. Hers was dirt and fresh air and organic veggies.

She'd been down this road before and it had ended in tears. Adrian and Cash might be very different men, but she'd dismissed the differences in the past. Was it wise to do so again?

She'd immersed herself so totally in Adrian's wealthy world she'd almost lost her identity. Would Cash expect the same from her? Or would he keep that part of his life separate from her, and end up alienating her that way?

'Hey, you've gone quiet,' he said. 'Surely you can tolerate not seeing me for one night?'

'It'll be tough, but I'll get by,' she said, knowing her dry response would get a laugh out of him.

'So I'll pick you up for the ball tomorrow at six?'

'I'll be ready,' she said, all too aware that was far from the case.

She'd never be ready to have the conversation she needed to with Cash.

'See you then, Cinders.' He made a smooching noise and hung up.

She pressed the mobile to her chest, wishing she could hold onto the feeling talking with Cash—being with Cash—elicited.

Unfortunately, as she knew better than most, not everything lasted for ever.

CHAPTER TWELVE

CASH HAD WRESTLED his bow tie into submission when the doorbell rang.

He glanced at his watch and frowned. Less than thirty minutes to pick up Lucy and head to the Melbourne Town Hall for the Valentine's Day ball. Which meant whoever was arriving on his doorstep unannounced would get marching orders.

He opened the door and his heart sank. Ivenka Shoor, Melbourne's top newsreader, might be one of his prime clients but their meetings were notoriously long. Not to mention dramatic.

Ivenka had a flair for turning the mundane into the extraordinary and he didn't have time for it now.

'Do you have a minute, Cash?' Ivenka didn't wait for his answer, pushing past him with the determination of a woman used to getting her own way.

'You'll have to make it quick. I'm on my way out.'

'Heading to the ball?' She gestured at her slinky black dress that did little to hide her figure. He might have been interested at one time but not any more. Right now, all Cash wanted to do was get to Lucy's ASAP.

'Yeah.'

'Me too, should be a blast.'

Trying to hide his impatience, Cash glanced at his

watch. 'Surely this can wait 'til morning? I really have to go—'

'That last investment you made on my behalf? My brother's doing something shonky with the dividends and I'm worried. I need your help.'

Crap. As much as Cash wanted to ditch Ivenka, he couldn't. She'd referred too many clients his way for him to shove her out of the door or defer this until the morning. He had to sort this now.

'Give me a minute and we'll get to the bottom of this.'

'Knew I could count on you.' She blew him a kiss. It made him inwardly cringe.

He headed into the study to grab his laptop, firing a quick apologetic text to Lucy and detour directions to the limo driver on the way. The faster he fixed Ivenka's latest crisis, the faster he could meet up with the woman he cared about.

Cash's laptop lay open on the desk and as he picked it up the screen flickered to life to display what he'd been working on.

But by the larger than life picture on the screen, he hadn't been working this afternoon. He'd been staring at a pic of Lucy gazing at him during the post-disco interview.

He knew the exact moment they'd cropped this still. At the end, when she'd been discussing her dream date.

Her vulnerability had surprised him at the time, but what hit him now was the way she was looking at him. As if she trusted him enough to divulge that kind of information.

The disco had been their first function and he'd been so gung-ho, trying to impress her. Trying to woo her too, considering their dance-floor kiss.

Yet staring at the picture now, it revealed more than

he could've thought possible. Because Lucy wasn't the only one caught off guard.

His expression, his body language, totally, one hundred per cent focused on her.

It came to him in a blinding flash of clarity.

He didn't just care about Lucy.

He loved her.

No woman had ever invaded his thoughts, and his dreams, as Lucy did.

She'd been on the fringe of his life for months now, yet it had taken some stupid PR stunt on his behalf to see the truth. That she was the kind of woman worth taking a risk on.

Blindsided, he rubbed his chest, unable to tear his gaze from the picture.

He loved Lucy.

Which begged the question: what the hell was he going to do about it?

Lucy wanted to make an impact tonight.

So she'd gone all out. Professional make-up, manicure, hair styled and a knockout dress she couldn't afford but had bought anyway.

She hadn't needed a stylist to tell her the dress would make an impression. A deep red satin sheath with a sweetheart neckline highlighted by crystals embedded in the bodice that draped her body and flattered in ways no control underwear could.

The colour brought out the new caramel highlights in her hair and made her eyes look impossibly huge.

She hoped Cash would take one look at her and want to keep her for real. He'd jokingly called her Cinders twice now but this girl had no intention of returning to a life of drudgery at midnight.

Uh-uh. At midnight, she hoped to be ensconced with Cash having a conversation about their future. Whatever that entailed.

Lucy twirled in front of the mirror one last time, revelling in the swish of fabric around her bare calves, the sheer indulgence of wearing shoes that sparkled.

She missed this. Missed the dressing up and the socialising and the joy of wearing fabulous clothes. She'd half expected to be panicky about donning her old persona: a woman who thrived on fashion and frivolity. A side of her she'd deliberately shut away as part of her defence mechanism against the pain Adrian had inflicted.

But freeing her inner romantic was liberating. She felt amazing, on top of the world, a woman who could do anything and be anything.

A woman confident in her capabilities to go after the guy she wanted. A woman ready to break free of the past once and for all and embrace the future.

Her mobile beeped at the same time she picked up her lip-gloss for a final swipe. One glance at the screen and she laid the gloss down. Just seeing Cash's name appearing on the screen made her heart ricochet in her chest.

She hit the message icon.

Sorry Luce
Client crisis in progress
Car will pick U up
Will C U @ ball

Her enthusiasm deflated as she stared at the screen in dismay.

She'd spent an inordinate amount of time getting ready for tonight. Had checked her make-up and teeth and hair a thousand times. Had practised wearing her new shoes to ensure they could dance the night away. Had checked all angles in the mirror on countless occasions in the last half-hour.

All because she'd wanted to make a dazzling first impression when she opened her front door to Cash.

She shouldn't feel so disillusioned, but she did. She felt as if she'd been robbed of her grand moment. She felt let down. And that told her more than she needed to know.

Cash mattered to her. His opinion mattered to her, and, while she'd see him soon enough, having him choose some stupid business over her rankled.

Bad enough she had a bunch of feelings careening out of control, now she could add disappointment to the mix. For the first time since her disastrous marriage, she was willing to take a chance on letting a guy into her heart.

And she'd hoped to let Cash know that tonight.

But to feel this crushed...had her feelings really moved beyond *like* and into *love*?

And if so, was she ready for it?

Lucy picked up the lip-gloss with a shaky hand and waited until it stopped trembling before applying a final coat.

She compressed her lips together, then puckered up at the mirror, perfectly rote motions before a night out.

But all the final touches in the world wouldn't change facts.

She might have fallen in love with Cash Burgess.

A guy who didn't do commitment.

Her hands started shaking again and she headed for the kitchen, where she poured herself a glass of Riesling and downed it in five gulps.

The alcohol burned her throat, she drank it that quick, but it was nothing compared to the burn of something stronger in her chest.

Needing more courage but knowing another glass of wine wasn't the answer, she re-corked. After twenty-five futile minutes of channel surfing, pacing the lounge and checking her reflection in the hallway mirror to ensure she looked okay, it was a relief when the doorbell rang.

Seeing Cash would settle her nerves. Or send them into orbit. As long as she didn't have a crash landing either way.

She opened the door to find a driver in a uniform with the PR company logo on his left breast pocket.

'Good evening, Miss Grant. I'm here to take you to the ball.'

Right sentiment. Wrong guy.

She forced a smile. 'Thanks.'

He stood back and waited as she slipped her phone into her evening bag, locked up and preceded him down the porch steps to the car.

The driver held open a back door and she slid into the leather confines of the limo, annoyed by the irrational sting of tears.

She shouldn't be this disappointed. Cash's work was important to him, she understood that. Heck, they wouldn't be together, fake or otherwise, if he weren't hell-bent on ensuring his business was front and centre.

So why did she feel like bawling as the driver closed the door, slipped behind the steering wheel and started the car?

He had the petition up, something she was eternally grateful for. She didn't want to make small talk. She didn't want to do much of anything but sit back and ponder whether she was overreacting.

If she had a client crisis, she would do everything in her power to fix the problem. Understandable Cash would do the same.

But she'd be lying to herself if she didn't admit being a teensy-weensy bit annoyed that he'd put work ahead of her on this important night.

It was the grand finale of their sham relationship and all indications pointed to him not wanting this to end as much as her.

She'd hoped to make a grand entrance with him at the ball, had hoped to prove to him she could be a part of his world.

She'd never felt so alive as she had this past week and Cash was a part of that. For her to be willing to take a risk, she'd been pretty damn sure he reciprocated her feelings.

Her doubts had been silenced following her chat with Gram yesterday. She'd seen the rock-solid relationship her grandparents had had, based on mutual respect and love. She wanted that. And knowing Gram might have been aware of Pops' foibles but loved him unconditionally went a long way to convincing Lucy that maybe it wasn't so bad taking a risk on following her heart if it felt right.

'We're here, miss.'

The driver stopped outside the Melbourne Town Hall, a glorious old building she loved for the architecture. As he held the door open her gaze landed on a flower vendor selling a gorgeous array of flowers and fruit nearby.

She loved this city, loved the many gardens surrounding the CBD. She couldn't live anywhere but the Garden State. Yet she suddenly knew in her heart that if Cash moved to Timbuktu she'd move there too to be with the man she loved.

The driver tipped his cap. 'Have a pleasant evening, miss.'

'Thanks.' Lucy mounted the stairs alongside fellow ball attendees, her earlier enthusiasm returning.

The rustle of silks, the smell of expensive fragrances, the gleam of cufflinks surrounded her and she swept into the foyer, eagerly scanning the crowd in search of her man.

It took her less than ten seconds to locate him, and two seconds to process what she was seeing.

Cash's client crisis involved a voluptuous TV presenter in a staggeringly low-cut black dress draped all over him, one hand resting on his chest, the other around his waist, while she gazed up at him in adoration.

And Cash was laughing, his head bent low to hear what the blonde was saying, their bodies pressed against each other.

The old Lucy would've turned and run, as she'd run after learning of Adrian's infidelities.

But the new Lucy had learned to harden her resolve over the years and wouldn't back down without a fight.

How many times had she seen pictures of Cash just like this—with some beautiful woman all over him—online when she'd Googled him after he'd first asked her to be his fake girlfriend?

Too many to count, considering it was his job to provide financial advice to the stars. Socialising was part of his job, his version of professional networking, so finding him here with a semi-famous woman shouldn't have been a shock.

What was shocking was the intense jealousy making her shake with every step that took her closer to the jocular couple.

Whatever he'd done, he'd averted the crisis. Too bad Lucy was now the one at risk of having a crisis of her own.

She dragged in calming breaths, flexing and unflexing her fingers the closer she got. It helped. Until she saw the blonde slip her hand underneath the lapel of Cash's tux jacket, an intimate gesture that he should've rebuffed. He didn't.

He caught sight of her at that moment and, rather than appearing guilty, he had the audacity to beam at her as if he'd been waiting for her all his life.

'Luce, come and meet Ivenka.' He slipped out from under the blonde's clutches to place a kiss on her cheek and draw her close to him.

She tried not to stiffen but he must've noticed the barest flinch, for he shot her a quick glance.

'Pleased to meet you.' Lucy held out her hand to the blonde, who hesitated before shaking it.

Looked as if Ivenka didn't return the sentiment, as she quickly excused herself and melted into the crowd.

'You look stunning.' He held her at arm's length, his sweeping stare starting at her toes and working upwards. 'Exquisite.'

'Thanks,' she said, wishing this could've happened at her house, with just the two of them, not with the after-effects of her jealousy making her want to say crazy things. Things like, *Do you really like me or are you a two-timing loser too?*

'Ready to go in?' He held out the crook of his elbow and she threaded her hand through it.

'Sure.'

They'd barely taken a step when Lucy blurted, 'Was the crisis averted?'

'Yeah.' He rolled his eyes. 'Ivenka's brother was siphoning her money. I managed to avert the prospect of lawyers and court.'

Lucy wanted to ask, 'And none of that could've waited 'til morning?' but she settled for, 'Glad you got it sorted.'

'Me too.' He paused and tilted her chin up so she had

no option but to look into those beautiful blue eyes she'd grown to love. 'Gives me all evening to focus on my gorgeous date.'

Not girlfriend. Fake or otherwise.

Date.

Yep, this evening was getting better by the minute. Lucy faked a smile. 'They're announcing the winners soon. We should get to our table.'

Confusion clouded his eyes but he didn't push it. 'Okay, Cinders, let's go in.'

As they entered the ballroom, complete with pink and red heart-shaped helium balloons tied to every surface, silver-foiled Cupids stuck everywhere and towering red rose centrepieces that made every table look like a hothouse, Lucy had a sneaking suspicion her Prince Charming might just be a pumpkin after all.

Cash did this for a living. Schmoozed and backslapped and listened to TV stars drone on, so consumed by their self-importance they didn't know when to stop.

He should be used to it but tonight he was off his game. His grand plans to romance Lucy in style had been shot. First with Ivenka's dramatic crisis when she'd arrived on his doorstep as he'd been getting ready for the ball, and now with the constant parade of well-wishers who wanted to shake his hand or pat him on the back because of his favourite status to win tonight.

He couldn't give a rat's ass who won tonight. He'd achieved his objective. Re-signing many old clients, holding onto those in danger of leaving him, and gaining some hugely positive PR for his company. He'd heard earlier today that the jilted starlet who'd threatened his reputation had left the country to try her luck in Hollywood.

Considering her B-grade acting skills, she was going to need that luck and plenty of it.

So he should have been flying tonight. But something had him on edge: Lucy's uncharacteristic coolness. Sure, she smiled and nodded and pretended to genuinely be interested in every person that came up to chat, but he could see the signs.

The slight angling of her body away from his.

The infrequent handholding.

The inability to meet his eyes for longer than a few seconds.

The subtle withdrawing with every smile fading too soon, her forced laughter at his jokes, the worry clouding her eyes when she thought he wasn't looking.

Was she preparing to revert to his gardener after tonight? Was that why she was behaving like this?

He had to reassure her, had to convince her how much she meant to him. The sooner they could slip out of this place, the better.

'Ladies and gentlemen, can I have your attention?' The PR firm's CEO waited for the crowd to quiet before continuing. 'Can I also have the competing couples move towards the front and line up below the stage?'

'Ready to strut your stuff one last time?' he said, holding out his hand to Lucy.

Her hesitation was imperceptible to all but the practised eye but he saw it, and his concern doubled.

'Let's do this.' She slipped her hand into his, its cold clamminess at odds with her usual warmth.

'You okay?' he murmured as they headed for the stage.

'Yeah.'

Her terse one-syllable response inspired him even less.

They waited at the bottom of the stage while the CEO droned on about the fun of romance and the importance of Valentine's Day and one lucky couple's dream date. And all the while, Lucy kept her gaze fixed on the CEO, not glancing his way even when he squeezed her hand.

Yep, something was seriously wrong.

'And now I'd like to announce the winner.' The CEO made a big show of opening a sealed envelope, when, if the online voting was anything to go by, they'd won by a landslide.

He'd looked forward to whisking Lucy away on a dream date, especially after tonight when he'd hoped to lay his heart on the line.

Now? He wasn't so sure.

The CEO cleared his throat. 'This couple won by a huge margin, earning the title of Most Romantic Valentine's Day Couple.'

He paused and rattled the envelope for dramatic effect. 'Congratulations to Cash Burgess and Lucy Grant. You win the Valentine's Day dream date, courtesy of GR8 4U Public Relations. Enjoy.'

A loud cheer went up as people wanting to hug and air-kiss and congratulate besieged them.

Cash tried his best to hold onto Lucy's hand but she slipped away in the sheer volume of people wanting to get closer to them.

He craned his neck, searching for her, and their gazes collided, hers quietly accepting of...? What? This mayhem?

This meant nothing, a momentary glitch before the real aim of the evening started: him getting her alone so they could talk about their future.

He smiled, hoping she'd understand that once this mayhem subsided they were out of here.

It must've lost something in the translation because

Lucy turned away, leaving him with a sick feeling in the pit of his stomach.

That talk with his dad yesterday had given him the confidence to pursue a relationship for the first time in his life.

But what if his judgement was as off as his dad's?

He'd always vowed there was no way he would open himself up for the kind of pain Ronnie had gone through after being rejected by his mum.

What if he already had?

'Could the Valentine's Day couples please take to the dance floor for a special dance?'

Lucy waited. Just as she'd waited for the last ten minutes while Cash shook hands and slapped backs and accepted kisses from countless women.

They'd been parted in the swarm rushing to congratulate them, but he hadn't come after her. Instead, she'd stood there and watched the man she loved in his element, surrounded by a bunch of fake schmoozers.

And now, as the other couples took to the dance floor and the first bars of a romantic ballad filled the air, Cash stood to one side, deep in conversation with his friend Barton.

Had he heard the MC's call? Did he even care?

That was when Lucy's brittle hold on her bad mood snapped.

She'd never liked being ignored, had put up with it from Adrian too many times to count. But she was done being anyone's wallflower.

She barged up to Cash, grinding her teeth with each step. Barton must've seen something in her expression because he excused himself and melted into the crowd by the time she reached Cash.

'Hey, there you are—'

'We have to do an obligatory dance, then I'm out of here,' she said, stopping short of shoving him in the chest for good measure.

For the first time since she'd met him, Cash stared at her, gobsmacked.

'Come on.' She jerked her head towards the dance floor where the other couples had already started swaying to a soppy nineties ballad. 'They're waiting for us.'

'Screw them,' he finally said, his expression wavering between outraged and confused. 'I want to know what's got into you.'

'Not now,' she said, lowering her voice when several people nearby glanced at them. 'Let's get this done.'

Lucy knew dancing would involve touching and, despite craving Cash's hands all over her for a week, she inadvertently flinched when he took her hand.

He swore under his breath and she totally agreed with the sentiment. This entire situation had been crappy from the start: fake relationship for the sake of monetary reward. Pity she'd been foolish enough to read more into it.

He threaded his fingers through hers and she sucked in a deep breath to quell the instinct to yank her hand away.

She could do this. She'd been good at pretending once. Pretending that Adrian's continual flirting with anything in a skirt didn't bother her, because he'd chosen her, married her. Pretending his long absences in the evening were work, not play. Pretending she was happy when in fact she'd soon grown tired of the high life and had craved what she'd wanted all along: someone to love her.

Now, all she had to do was get through this winners' dance and she could leave. She'd talk to Cash tomorrow, when her resentment had waned and she'd had a chance to calm down.

Because right now, she could quite happily hit him over the head with a shovel for being so clueless.

The crowd applauded as they reached the dance floor and Cash gave a theatrical little bow that annoyed her even more. When they reached the middle, he took her into his arms and stared into her eyes, as if she were the only woman in the world.

As if.

Seeing Cash interact with his peers here tonight had given her a much-needed dose of reality. Cash might be a nice guy but she didn't belong in his world and had no desire to try and fit in.

She wanted to spend her thirties with a guy she loved, curled up on the couch watching movies and laughing at in-jokes. She wanted to go out to dinner to favourite restaurants, and walk in the Botanical Gardens on Sunday and have brunch by the Yarra.

What she didn't want was parties and schmoozing and a world where glitz was valued more than niceness.

Cash danced as he did everything else in his well-ordered life: with polish and precision. When she faltered, he covered for her. Not surprising, with her rigid back and tense posture. But he didn't miss a step and his poise exacerbated the distance between them.

'I know this week has been rough but we're almost done,' he said, lowering his head to murmur in her ear. 'Just a few more hours, that's all.'

She accidentally trod on his toes but this time she didn't let him cover for her. She stepped away, what she should've done before they'd got this far. 'A few more hours? Are you out of your mind?'

Frowning, he glanced around, and she had her answer right there. He was more concerned with what people thought than how she was feeling.

'Cash, these are your friends, your peers. You stay.'

He shook his head, as if not quite comprehending what he was hearing. 'You're actually leaving?'

'That's what I said before that stupid final dance, but you weren't listening.'

And with the gulf widening between them now their week was done, he never would.

Determined to make a classy exit before she blubbered, she forced a stiff smile. 'Enjoy the rest of your evening.'

With Cash speechless for the second time in ten minutes, she headed for the door.

Fresh air would help. It always did. How many dawn mornings had she leaned on her shovel in someone's garden and just breathed? Willing the pain away, wishing the memories would fade faster.

It had taken her nine years to get to this point: strong, independent, happy.

Though that wasn't entirely true. She'd been happier this last week than she had in ages and she had Cash to thank for that.

He'd made her feel alive.

Yet how she was feeling now? Like a wilting daisy that had been opened to a powerful sun, folding in on itself, back to self-preservation mode.

She exited the town hall and stood on the top step, dragging in great lungfuls of air. Not quite what she'd envisaged, considering the slight smog that hung over inner city Melbourne, but air all the same.

Stupid thing was, now she'd escaped, she didn't know what to do. Should she hail a taxi and head home? But that wouldn't make Cash look good, considering that was why he'd done this in the first place, for the positive PR.

That was when reality slammed into her with the force of a runaway backhoe.

Their week was officially over. Better for him, they'd won, ensuring a stack of good PR.

Maybe she wasn't useful any longer?

Was that what his behaviour back there had been about? She'd outgrown her usefulness and his subtle withdrawing was a way of letting her down gently?

Maybe the romantic fantasy she'd built up in her head, of the two of them being a real couple beyond this week, had been just that? A stupid fantasy.

'Hey, where are you tearing off to?' Cash's hand clamped on her shoulder and he spun her around. 'What's got into you tonight?'

'Nothing.' She shrugged off his hand, hating the way his mouth compressed into an angry line.

'You bolting out of there sure didn't look like nothing to me.'

'I think I'll head home—'

'Are you serious? We just won that competition. They expect us to—'

'To what? Keep faking it for everyone?'

He paled. 'I thought we'd moved past that a few days ago.'

Lucy's heart faltered. Maybe she was overreacting? Then she remembered the utter desolation of standing in that exquisite ballroom, surrounded by a bunch of strangers, watching the guy she loved ignore her as she came in a distant second to everything else.

She wouldn't put up with it. Never again.

'I did too. But after what happened in there?' She jerked her head towards the hall. 'I don't think so.'

Confusion creased his brow. 'What happened in

there? We won an amazing dream date. I thought you'd be happy.'

'Things don't impress me.' She wrapped her arms around her middle to ward off the chill seeping through her. 'People do.'

'I don't get it.'

'And that's half the problem.' She shook her head. 'We come from different worlds, Cash. It's never going to work.'

'Bull.' He reached out to her and she held him off with a raised hand. 'Maybe I'm no good at this relationship stuff but I'm willing to give it a go. What about you?'

Lucy should be ecstatic he cared enough to want to explore what they'd started this week. It was what she'd wanted.

Until this moment, when she knew with a startling clarity deep in her heart she could never put up with standing on the outskirts looking in.

It had been a deep-seated insecurity that she'd acknowledged once her marriage to Adrian imploded. She'd spent too much time at functions on the fringes, watching him charm everyone.

She'd found it endearing at the time, her husband's popularity. And she'd supported him unconditionally wherever they went.

But watching Cash do something similar in that ballroom showed her how far she'd come over the years.

Simply, she couldn't go through that again.

It wasn't Cash's fault, wasn't a deliberate ploy to ostracise her. It was a guy doing what he'd always done, and not willing to change because he had someone special in his life.

She shook her head. 'Sorry, I can't do this.'

Stony-faced, he stared at her in disbelief. 'None of this

makes any bloody sense. You led me to believe…' His jaw clamped shut, anger making his neck muscles pop.

'What?'

'That I was more to you than a means for money,' he spat out, glaring at her with so much fury she almost cried.

But tears were for sissies and Cash's wild accusation lit a fuse to her temper.

'Considering that money's all that matters to you, I don't see why you'd care,' she said, resisting the urge to shake some sense into him. 'I need that money to save my gram's house. What's your excuse?'

She snapped her fingers. 'That's right. Accumulating wealth is an occupational habit for shallow, narcissistic men who see a big bank balance as a status symbol. Image is everything and you'll do anything to get what you want, including pay someone to be your *girlfriend*.'

She couldn't stop, her inner resentment spilling out in a torrent. Every worry she'd harboured about him, every insecurity of hers, coalesced into this shocking moment that left them both reeling.

She knew she'd gone too far the moment the harsh words tumbled from her mouth. She wished she could take them back when he paled and stood stock-still, not even blinking.

'Cash, I'm sorry—'

'No you're not.' His flat, emotionless monotone scared her as much as his blank expression. 'Good to know what you think of me. But you want to know something? I'd rather have clear goals in my life than not having any ambition and settling for a life of nothing because of some crap that happened in the past.'

Lucy stared at the man she'd thought she loved, wondering how she could have got it so wrong. Again.

Sorrow clogged her throat and she swallowed several times before responding. 'I'm happy being a gardener. It's not *nothing.*' She jabbed a finger in his direction. 'And you know nothing about my marriage so shut the hell up.'

She scored a direct hit as remorse flickered in his eyes. 'I know that whatever happened back then has made you into the woman you are today, scared to take a risk because you may get hurt again.'

Not willing to have this conversation with him, Lucy shook her head. 'You don't know anything about me.'

She hiked up her skirt in one hand and carefully descended the steps, a small part of her wishing he'd come after her.

He didn't and as a taxi miraculously appeared in front of her she quickly got in and gave her address to the driver.

Lucy willed herself not to look back, but as the taxi slid away from the kerb she glanced out of the window. Cash's stricken pallor almost as cold as the town hall he was silhouetted against as he stood alone, hands thrust into his pockets, a devastatingly handsome man in a tux without the woman who'd been willing to give him everything.

CHAPTER THIRTEEN

BY EIGHT THE next morning, Cash had fielded three phone calls from new clients, responded to five emails and watched an investment he'd made in a new company just launched on the New York stock exchange make four of his oldest clients very rich.

It should've been a good day.

The commission he'd earn from the new clients, most of them gained through socialising last night, would be huge, and the connections he'd made would ensure that his company remained intact.

Everything he'd worked so hard for, saved.

Yeah, this should be a great day.

Instead, all the money in the world couldn't fix his crappy mood.

Only one woman could do that and she'd made it abundantly clear what she thought of him.

How the hell had he got it so wrong with Lucy?

He swept a stack of papers off his desk as Barton stuck his head around the study door.

'Bad time?'

'Yeah,' Cash growled, wishing he could tell his best mate to rack off. No point ruining two relationships in twelve hours.

'Tough. We need to celebrate.' Bart strode into his

study and dumped a stack of newspapers on his desk. 'I know you've probably seen these online but never hurts to keep paper relics of your greatest successes.'

Cash pinched the bridge of his nose, wishing the dull ache that had resided there since last night would vanish. 'I take it your company is pleased with the outcome of the Valentine's Day couple crap?'

'Crap?' Bart's eyebrows shot up. 'I thought you and Lucy were right into it.'

'You knew it was fake from the start,' he said, his bitterness audible. 'I got what I wanted, so did she.'

Bart's eyes crinkled in confusion. 'But you two...I mean, it looked like...'

'Appearances can be deceiving,' Cash said, pushing back from his desk to cross his office and stare out of the window. At the garden that would soon be refurbished. By Lucy, strutting around here every day.

Hell.

'Sure they can, which is why I thought you two weren't faking it at the end.'

Cash heard the rustle of newspaper, before Bart said, 'Here. Take a look at this.'

The last thing Cash wanted to see was anything remotely connected to Lucy, but the faster he acquiesced to Bart's demands, the faster he could get rid of him.

'What is it?'

'A recap of your hot and heavy romance with the luscious Lucy.' Bart held up a broadsheet, covered from top to bottom with pictures of him and Lucy taken over the last week.

Lucy hand-feeding him strawberries at the picnic.

Lucy's arms looped around his neck as he carried her off the skating rink.

Lucy's lips locked on his at the disco.

And many more, each pic depicting a happy, smiling, laughing Lucy. With him looking like a smitten, devoted schmuck.

'Looks pretty real to me,' Bart said, shoving the newspaper into his hands. 'So why are you feeding me a load of BS that says otherwise?'

'Because it's not real...' Cash said, trailing off when he caught sight of a small picture, tucked away at the bottom, right-hand corner of the page.

It was the same still he'd seen on his computer before the ball. The picture that had made him realise he loved her.

So what had happened last night to make Lucy change from an adoring woman who appeared to be in love to a raving shrew who despised him and all he stood for?

'If that's not real, I'll pose as your Valentine's Day date next year,' Bart said, swallowing a guffaw when Cash shot him a death glare.

'This isn't funny.' Cash folded the newspaper and threw it on his desk. Yeah, as if that could erase those happy snaps from his mind.

'Sure it is.' Bart smirked. 'Never thought I'd see the day when a woman brought you to your knees, you big dufus. No one can fake looking like that. Looking like they're in love.'

'I'm not in l—'

Bart sniggered. 'Yeah, keep telling yourself that, big guy. In the meantime, in case you waste any more time stewing over whatever has you in a snit, don't forget it's Valentine's Day. *The* perfect day for grovelling.' Bart shrugged. 'If there's a need to, that is. Just saying.'

So Bart had a point.

Through all the confusion of the last week—faking

it at the events, revealing glimpses of their true selves, falling into bed—one fact remained steady.

Cash loved Lucy.

Was he going to throw the first real relationship he'd ever had away because Lucy had got spooked and deliberately pushed him away?

Last night, he'd been angry. She'd hurt him.

But in the cold light of day, with visual evidence of their developing relationship laid out in print, Cash knew he couldn't walk away.

Not without a damn good fight.

He held out his hand. 'Thanks, Bart.'

'No worries, mate.' Bart pumped his hand. 'Just one last thing.'

'What?'

'Convince Lucy to let me be your best man, 'cause I don't think she likes me very much.'

Cash laughed. 'If she takes me back, you're on.'

Gram arrived at nine the morning after the ball, took one look at Lucy's face and bustled into the kitchen.

She didn't offer any words of advice or any platitudes, heading straight for the coffee plunger and the pantry instead.

Lucy had been through this before and was eternally grateful Gram would stay in the background, bake up a storm and be here when she was ready to talk.

Which wasn't now.

Six hours later, Lucy had aerated her front and back lawns, had re-mulched the veggie patch, replanted three borders, trimmed hedges and tidied the compost heap.

When she finally stopped and sank onto the front step, Gram bustled out, freshly squeezed lemonade in one hand, a plate of double-choc-chip cookies in the other.

'Thanks.' Lucy sculled two glasses of lemonade and scoffed five cookies before some of her energy returned.

'You're welcome.' Gram sat next to her and nibbled on a cookie.

Lucy had no idea how long they sat there like that, but as she hugged her knees to her chest and rested her chin on top she was eternally grateful for Gram's silent support.

Lucy wanted to talk. She wanted to tell Gram all about her horrid night but the hurt was too fresh, too raw. And without any sleep, followed by a day of relentless physical labour, Lucy knew she'd bawl if she started talking about Cash now.

'I'll be heading off soon, love, but I've left a fruitcake and banana bread cooling on the stove, and there are lamingtons and brownies stored in the pantry.'

For the first time all day, Lucy felt like smiling. Sounded like Gram had worked off her concern by baking.

'Thanks, Gram, you're the best.' Lucy laid her head on Gram's shoulder and fought the urge to cry again when Gram slipped an arm around her waist.

'Whatever you need, whenever you need it, I'm here for you.' Gram kissed the top of her head.

Lucy closed her eyes, catapulted back in time to the two of them doing this very thing: Pops making himself scarce when Lucy had turned up at their house in tears, proclaiming her marriage was over.

Gram had sat her down, wrapped her arms around her, and just let her be.

Lucy had shut down for a week back then, not coming out of her old room, barely touching food. Until she'd told her grandparents everything and had set about rebuilding a new life.

The events of the last week weren't so life changing but Cash had hurt her just the same. She'd opened her heart to him and he'd broken it without a backward glance.

Not by anything he did, but by what he didn't do. Somehow, that made it all the harder to accept.

Lucy heard a car pull up and an engine idling, followed by a door slam.

She opened her eyes to see Cash striding up her path, determination lengthening his strides.

Gram eased away, stood and patted her shoulder. 'I'll be inside if you need me.'

Lucy wanted to say 'stay' but she couldn't unglue her tongue from the roof of her mouth.

When she'd envisaged her next meeting with Cash, it was to be on her terms: at his house, with her brusque and businesslike commencing work on his garden. She hadn't imagined he'd be looking incredibly poised in a signature pinstriped suit with a sky-blue shirt that accentuated his eyes, and her in grungy khaki shorts, tank top and steel-capped work boots.

Swiping her hands on the side of her shorts, she stood, every muscle protesting after being pushed too hard. 'What are you doing here?'

'Picking you up for our dream date.' He stopped at the bottom step and looked up at her. 'And I'm not taking no for an answer.'

She barked out a laugh. 'You're crazy. Look at me.' She pointed at her grimy clothes. 'Even if I wanted to go with you, which I don't, do I look like I'm dressed for a fancy date?'

He looked her straight in the eye and said, 'I like you just the way you are.'

Of all the possible things he could've said, of all

the apologies, it was the one that held the most weight with her.

She felt she didn't belong in his world. Yet he wanted to take her out looking like this?

'The limo driver won't be impressed.'

He raised an eyebrow. 'Since when do you care what other people think?'

'You do,' she said, the accusation slipping out before she could censor it.

Weariness accentuated the lines at the corners of his mouth as his shoulders slumped slightly. 'Yeah, but after listening to a wise woman last night I'm starting to re-evaluate my priorities.'

Wow, another admission that went a long way to swaying Lucy.

She hovered on the top step, torn between wanting to take one last chance on hearing what Cash had to say and staying safe, protecting her heart.

The screen door creaked open and Gram stepped up behind her. Gram leaned closer to whisper in her ear, 'Go. Don't let the demons of the past stop you from taking a risk on a wonderful future.'

It was the final push Lucy needed and she spun around, giving Gram an impulsive hug, before turning back to Cash and nodding.

'Okay. Let's go.'

Cash beamed. 'Thanks. You must be Lucy's infamous Gram? Pleased to meet you.' He shook Gram's hand as Gram practically simpered.

'And you must be the dashing young charmer who has swept my granddaughter off her feet.'

'Guilty as charged, though you flatter me,' he said, laughing. 'I'll make sure she gets home safe and sound before curfew.'

Lucy rolled her eyes at his tongue-in-cheek declaration.

'Why not stay out all night?' Gram said, with a wink, and Lucy blushed.

Cash held out his hand to her and after the slightest hesitation she took it, the familiar tingle whenever he touched her making her want to fling herself into his arms and never let go.

He raised it to his lips and kissed the back of her hand. 'Promise you'll never leave me standing alone again.'

Lucy almost melted all over the garden path. 'Sorry, I don't make promises I can't keep.'

'Well then, guess that gives me something to work on during this date.' He waved the driver back into the limo and opened the back door for her. 'Because, Luce? I intend to make this a date you'll never forget.'

Lucy slid into the back of the limo, her goal to emotionally extricate herself from Cash under threat by his ability to say the right thing.

It was part of his practised charm; she understood that. What she didn't understand was her irrational urge to give in to him again, despite hardening her heart after their fall-out last night.

'You know I'm not feeling the love after last night, right?'

'Yeah, I kinda got that impression when you ditched me at the ball.' He slid in behind her, closed the door, angled his body towards her and draped his arm across the headrest, appearing way too relaxed while she churned inside. 'And I'm glad you deigned to go on this date with me, considering you think I'm shallow and narcissistic.'

'Ouch.' She winced. 'I was kinda mad. But you're no saint. You accused me of leading a life of nothing.'

He puffed out a breath. 'I think we both said things we didn't mean.'

He held up his hands, palm up, no tricks up those sleeves. 'How about we clear the air so we can enjoy this date?'

Lucy wanted to agree. She wanted to wipe the slate clean and pretend last night hadn't happened. She wanted to allow this incredible guy to charm his way into her good graces again.

But her hard-learned self-preservation over the years had kicked in in a big way when Cash had virtually ignored her last night.

She wouldn't play this game with him. Not now, not ever.

'Were you jealous?'

She shot him a death glare. 'Of?'

Suitably sheepish, he shrugged. 'When you arrived and saw me talking to Ivenka, you looked seriously pissed.'

'Talking? Is that what you call it when a woman's draped all over you?' Lucy hadn't meant to sound shrewish but that was exactly how her judgemental observation came out.

Like any guy with half an ego, Cash grinned, and she wanted to whack him. 'Ivenka is a client, that's it.' He paused, adding almost as an afterthought, 'The women I socialise with are used to…ah, how shall I put this? Using their feminine wiles to get whatever they want.'

'Meaning they sleep their way to obtaining their goal, whatever that may be,' Lucy said drily, feeling like yesterday's rubbish in her grubby clothes when remembering Ivenka's designer dress.

'Basically? Yeah. Doesn't mean I'll ever fall for it.'

She cocked her head to one side, assessing his sincerity. 'So you're telling me you've never been involved with one of those stunning stars you advise?'

He had the grace to blush. 'I'm not a saint, Luce. I've never had a committed relationship and if a beautiful woman wants to extend the evening past dinner, I haven't always declined.'

Lucy fixed on the one thing he'd said that should send her running for the hills. 'Never had a committed relationship?'

He nodded. 'Let's just say my faith in the fairer sex isn't the best.'

Curious in spite of herself, she said, 'Why?'

'Probably all very Freudian. You know about my mum.'

'Yeah, but not every woman is like your mother.'

'Just like not every guy is like your jerk ex.'

'Touché.'

He glanced out of the window, lost in his thoughts for a moment. 'Guess I've never met a woman worth taking a risk for.'

'Relationships are risky, I'll give you that.'

'Until now,' he added, with a pointed stare in her direction.

Lucy's heart gave a traitorous leap. 'What?'

'I've never met a woman worth taking a risk for 'til now.'

He leaned forward and she shrank back into the furthest corner of the limo. 'Surely you know I'm crazy about you, Luce?'

Lucy had wished for this scenario several times over the last week but now the moment had arrived, the gloss had been taken off by her fears.

Fear of the future. Fear of taking a risk. Fear of being hurt again.

'Can we take a step back before last night? Before we both went a little crazy?'

She shook her head. 'If I've learned anything it's to not look back.'

He allowed her to wallow a little before changing tack.

'Tell me about your marriage.'

Her relationship with Adrian was the last thing she felt like discussing but she knew where he was going with this. He hoped to get insight into her past and use that to influence her decision now. It wouldn't work, but he'd told her about his family, the least she could do was reciprocate, considering she'd be seeing him daily for a while yet while landscaping his garden.

'I married young. Twenty-one. He swept me off my feet.'

He waited for her to continue, as if he had all the time in the world.

'My folks died in a car crash when I was a toddler. My grandparents raised me. I had a great life but money wasn't plentiful.'

He nodded. 'Know what you mean.'

She liked that about him, the fact he was willing to acknowledge his poor past, and how hard he'd worked to become a self-made millionaire.

'Then I met Adrian and my world changed. He was wealthy, old family money, and he swept me into his world.'

Cash's eyes narrowed, but not before she'd glimpsed a spark of jealousy.

'The classic whirlwind courtship. We married after six months.' She huffed out a breath. 'A year later I found out he'd been screwing around on me for most of my marriage. So I left.'

'Bastard,' he muttered, his hands fisted as if he wanted to punch something. 'Hope you took him for everything he was worth.'

Lucy shook her head. 'Not my style. I didn't want anything to remind me of my foolishness in falling for him, so I left it all behind.'

She couldn't contain a wistful sigh. 'Have to admit, I loved the finer things. The designer fashion, the expensive make-up, regular spa treatments. It was all divine...' Her resolve hardened. 'But not worth the price to put up with his infidelities.'

'Good for you.' He searched her face, as if unsure of her reaction to what he'd say next. 'Are you scared I'll treat you like Adrian did? Is that why you're holding out on me?'

'You're nothing like him,' she said, her vehemence startling both of them. 'Though last night, when you were busy schmoozing, it felt like I was having a flashback... Adrian used to treat me like a possession, something to trot out at functions but pay little attention to. Guess I felt like that with you last night.'

Cash swore. 'I never meant to ignore you—'

'I know, but that's exactly my point.' She gestured between them. 'You and I? We're worlds apart. I like dirt under my fingernails, you probably get a male mani every fortnight.'

She'd scored a direct hit by the tightening around his mouth.

'I like quiet nights at home on the sofa watching classic movies, you like attending premieres and clubs and partying for a living.'

'That's what I do, it's not who I am,' he said, so softly she had to lean closer to hear it.

'How would I know, when that's the only side of you I see?' Though that wasn't entirely true. She'd seen many facets to this intriguing man over the last week and she'd be doing him a disservice to dismiss him as one-dimensional.

'I'm not used to letting anyone see the real me,' he said, his steady gaze imploring her to listen. 'But I'm willing to take that risk with you. All I'm asking is that you do the same.'

Lucy wanted to say yes. She wanted to fling herself into his arms and kiss him silly. She wanted to be swept off her feet in style and be part of his world, just as she wanted him to be a part of hers.

But her doubts held her back.

'Can I have some time to think about it?'

Disappointment flashed across his face before he quickly masked it. 'Sure. Though I expect an answer by the time we reach our destination.'

She rolled her eyes. 'Where are we going anyway? I thought the prize said a posh dinner in a fancy restaurant at a winery on the peninsula?'

'You'll see,' he said, his grin infuriatingly smug. 'You'll also see that we're right for each other, despite your doubts.'

Lucy remained silent on that particular point, and as the limo left the city behind and headed towards the nearby hills fatigue overtook her.

Lucy finally slept for the first time in over twenty-four hours.

While Cash watched her, willing to wait for the woman he loved to come to her senses.

CHAPTER FOURTEEN

LUCY HAD THE most marvellous dream.

She'd been whisked away from her garden by a gorgeous guy who accepted her for who she was and wanted to be with her.

She woke to find the dream guy shaking her gently, his face temptingly close, his spicy aftershave enveloping her in warmth and excitement.

'We're here, Sleeping Beauty.' He slanted a soft kiss across her lips, the barest of touches over before it had begun.

She stretched. 'How long was I out for?'

'Fifty minutes.' His fingertip traced the skin under her eyes. 'No sleep last night, huh?'

'What gave it away? The puffy dark circles under my eyes making me look like a panda?'

'You always look beautiful to me,' he said, kissing her again, a little more forceful this time, leaving her gasping for air and certainly awake. 'I didn't sleep a wink. I figured you would've been the same.'

She nodded, grateful when the driver opened the back door and broke the intimacy. So what if Cash was astute enough to be clued in to her feelings? He wasn't so clued in last night at the ball when he'd left her alone while he mingled with his crowd.

'Uh-oh, you've got that look again.'

'What look?'

'The look you had before you fell asleep.' He touched between her brows. 'Like you weren't sure whether you wanted to slap me or castrate me.'

She smiled. 'You're safe. For now.'

He crossed his legs and grimaced.

'Where are we?' She stepped from the limo and glanced around, captivated by the surroundings.

They were in a private garden that resembled an urban forest. Beautifully manicured lawn bisected by curving sandstone paths, with some of her favourite plants strategically placed. Her landscaper's eye noticed how the designer had used Japanese blood grass, Maidenhair fern, black Mondo, Sansevieria and Liriope. It was her type of place and a much better venue than any fancy restaurant.

'There's more.' He took her hand without asking this time and led her down a narrow paved path that wound on the garden outskirts, before it stopped at a dead-end hedge. 'Through here.'

He touched an invisible door in the hedge that swung open, to reveal paradise.

As dusk fell over Melbourne the city's lights flickered to life, glittering like fairy dust against an ermine cape, many miles away.

It felt as if they were on top of the world, the spectacular view rivalled only by the expectant expression of the man beside her.

'We're on top of Mount Dandenong?'

He nodded. 'And your dinner awaits.'

He led her to a towering eucalypt in the far corner of the garden, where she spied a red and white checked picnic blanket spread under the tree, covered with a staggering amount of food.

He pointed to it. 'Salmon rosti, chicken and avocado crustless sandwiches, curried egg vol-au-vents, pâté, blue-vein cheese, raspberry and white chocolate muffins and the finest French champagne.'

He executed a little bow that made her giggle. 'All your favourites, if I'm not mistaken?'

More than a little impressed, she gestured at the picnic. 'You did all this?'

Surprisingly bashful, he nodded. 'I wanted this to be your dream date, not some highfalutin generic date that anyone could've gone on.'

That was when the significance of the venue and the picnic hit her. 'You remembered what I said in that interview?'

'Yeah, I listened. And remembered.' He rubbed the back of his neck, as if uncomfortable with her scrutiny. 'I think that was the moment I first fell for you.'

Lucy liked seeing Cash uncomfortable and a little vulnerable. It meant he was as unsure of his feelings as she was.

Not that she was getting her hopes up, but his honest declarations in the limo had gone some way to soothing her resentment from last night.

And organising her dream date meant the week they'd spent together hamming it up for the cameras had actually meant something to him too. That post-disco interview had been about playing it up for an audience, but he'd been intuitive enough to see through the flirty fibs to the one truth she'd uttered.

Shallow guys didn't do that kind of thing. They barely remembered how she liked her coffee, let alone something important like how she wanted to be wooed.

'So tell me the other moments you fell for me.' She

patted the picnic blanket next to her and he sat. 'And don't skimp on the details.'

His lips curved into the devastating smile she loved so much. 'I think the moment I was really smitten was when you took that spectacular tumble at the roller-skating rink.'

She screwed up her nose. 'I looked like an idiot.'

'Maybe a little?' He held up his thumb and forefinger an inch apart and she whacked him on the arm. 'It was more the way I felt watching you fall.' He tapped his chest directly over his heart. 'I got this weird burning feeling right here.'

'Probably from those beef nachos you scoffed before we laced up our skates.'

'You always do that.' His fingertip traced the contour of her cheek and she unwittingly held her breath. 'Hide your true feelings behind quips.'

Damn, there he went again, honing in on the real her. It unnerved her, his ability to switch from confident financier to intuitive boyfriend material.

'You don't know anything about my true feelings,' she said, hating how her brusque reply made the teasing sparkle in his eyes fade.

'I'd like to.' He took hold of her hand and she resisted the urge to yank it away.

She hated her hands. Hated the perpetual dry skin no matter how many lotions she tried. Hated the ragged cuticles. Hated the short, chipped nails.

They might be a testament to how hard she worked but, with Cash studying them and skimming a fingertip along the veins on the back of her hand, she felt inadequate.

'Tell me what you're thinking,' he said, raising her hand to his lips to gently brush kisses along her knuckles.

'You don't want to know,' she muttered, unable to stop a soft, wistful sigh.

'I do.' He lowered her hand but didn't release it. 'Call me corny, but I've never felt the way you make me feel and I don't want to lose you. So whatever it takes for me to make up for last night, or whatever I can do to convince you we have a future, I'll do it.'

She shook her head, battling the urge to bawl. 'It's not that simple—'

'Yeah, it is.'

With his tender, unwavering stare boring into her, silently pleading with her to give them a chance, she finally relented.

'I'm scared.'

Of all the responses she could've given, he obviously hadn't been expecting that one if his widening eyes were any indication.

'Of?'

'Scared our differences will ultimately drive us apart. Scared of us having a real relationship, only to have it fall apart. Scared of...' She swallowed the rest of her response. There was honesty and there was honesty.

Articulating how she felt? Would only complicate matters when she inevitably let him down.

'Tell me.' He squeezed her hand. 'All of it.'

Lucy had taken many risks in her life. Leaving a comfortable marriage. Starting afresh in a new job. Taking a loan for her own house.

But those risks paled in comparison to telling Cash the whole truth.

'Most of all, I'm scared of how much I feel for you,' she said, so softly he leaned towards her. 'And it can't be real, because we've only been dating for a week, and that was fake, and it's ridiculous because I don't believe in romance or any of that crap—'

'Then I think it's time you start believing.' He placed a finger against her lips to silence her. 'I did.'

Confused, Lucy said, 'Believe in me?'

'Believe in me.' He released her hand to extend his arms behind him and prop. 'I spent too many years as a kid trying to gain the approval of my old man by accumulating cash. The more I gave him, the happier he seemed to be.'

Cash shook his head. 'Though happy is too strong a word for what my dad was back then. Less unhappy is probably more accurate.'

Lucy heard the underlying sadness in his voice and yearned to put her arms around him. 'I'm sorry for what you went through.'

'I'm not.' He shook his head. 'Because every day I've worked my ass off over the years, relying on money as my security blanket, has taught me something.'

Blown away by his honesty, Lucy waited for him to continue.

'That all the money in the world, no matter how big my business, no matter how many clients I woo and impress, it all means nothing if I don't have what I want the most.'

Too afraid to ask, Lucy took a few deep breaths before saying, 'What's that?'

He looked her directly in the eye, his gaze unwavering. 'You.'

Lucy's chest ached with the enormity of his declaration, but she still had no idea what to say.

He delved in his pocket and pulled out a small pale blue box that made her heart falter. 'Happy Valentine's Day, Luce.'

In the devastating aftermath of last night, she'd forgotten today was Valentine's Day. Not that she ever noted the date considering what she thought of it, but with the memorable lead-up to this one she should've remembered.

She stared at the box, too scared to touch it. The implications of accepting that box and opening it were too terrifying to contemplate.

'Is that a…?' She cleared her throat, unable to speak past the giant lump of emotion.

He smiled as he flipped the lid open, the tenderness in his eyes making her tear up. Until she caught sight of the ring, a three-carat marquise diamond in white gold. Simple. Elegant. Stunning. The type of ring to define all rings.

'In case you were wondering, it's a ring for that finger.' He took the third finger on her left hand and wiggled it. 'And it means exactly what you think it means.'

He knelt in the dewy grass, slipped the ring out of the box and held her left hand. 'I'm not very good at this stuff, Luce, but with you by my side I'm willing to give it a shot.'

He held the ring over the tip of her finger. 'I love you, Cinders. Will you marry me?'

Lucy didn't feel like Cinderella. She felt like the luckiest woman in the world.

But she'd been here before: the ring, the proposal, the whirlwind romance.

Last time, she'd made the biggest mistake of her life by accepting a proposal after six months. What disaster would befall her this time after knowing the guy properly for only a week?

'We barely know each other,' she whispered, her hands shaking the longer he held that ring there. 'It's too soon, we're too different—'

'So you keep saying, but I'm not buying it.' He held her gaze, beseeching her to listen. 'The way I feel when I'm with you? Like nothing or no one else matters. I can be myself. And I love that you can be yourself around me. I love the dirt smudges on your nose and your funny boot tan lines on your legs and the way you happily walk around without artifice. But most of all? I love you for you. Every beautiful inch, inside and out.'

Speechless, and barely able to see through her tears, Lucy watched the man she loved slip the exquisite diamond onto her finger, all the way to the knuckle.

'That settles it,' he said, standing to bundle her into his arms.

'Technically I didn't say yes,' she said, unable to keep her joy from showing with an ear-splitting grin.

'You didn't have to. I can see your answer here.' He cupped her chin and stared into her eyes. 'You love me. Never in doubt.'

She could've taken him down a peg or two for his cockiness or berated him for bullying her into accepting the ring.

Instead, she looped her arms around her fiancé's neck, tugged his head down, and kissed him.

By the time they came up for air, darkness had descended and they could barely see the picnic blanket.

Didn't matter. Lucy wasn't terribly hungry.

At least, not for food.

EPILOGUE

Lucy elbowed her husband in the ribs. 'Are you seeing this or is it just me?'

Cash glanced over at the newly installed gazebo in his garden and nodded. 'Yep. I think my dad and your gram are getting it on.'

'*Euw*, that's disgusting,' Lucy said, smiling regardless. 'They're not getting it on, they're chatting. And maybe flirting a little.'

Cash slid an arm around her waist and hugged her tight. 'Guess our wedding day is spreading the love.'

She snuggled into him. 'Who would've thought that crappy, overcommercialised day could've brought us to this point?'

'Nothing wrong with Valentine's Day.' He nuzzled her neck. 'Especially when that little chubby guy with the bow and arrow had a hand in giving me the privilege of doing this every night.' He groped her butt and she yelped.

'Cupid had nothing to do with it,' she said, returning the favour and delighting in seeing his eyes twinkle with mischief. 'It was your stupid PR scheme that got us together.'

'Stupid?' He playfully tugged on her veil. 'Got you this far, didn't it?'

She released him and held up her left hand, the shiny white-gold wedding band catching the sunlight along with her marquise diamond. 'I still can't believe you slipped that ring on my finger after a week.'

He gestured at himself. 'Who could resist this? You were putty in my hands from that first date.'

'That eighties disco?' She scoffed. 'Took me a while longer to fall for your questionable charms.'

'Liar,' he murmured, kissing away any further objections she might have.

'Hey, you two, quit canoodling,' Gram called across the garden. 'Time to cut the cake.'

'Plenty of time to continue the *canoodling* later,' Cash said, snagging her hand and raising it to his lips. 'Because as beautiful as your dress is, I can't wait to get it off you.'

Lucy glanced down at her satin princess dress covered in a smattering of crystals with a metre train, wondering if she should pinch herself for the umpteenth time today.

Being a second marriage, she could've gone for simple and unpretentious.

But she loved this man with all her heart and wanted to embrace the old her, the girl who secretly loved romance and frivolity and fabulous fashion, so she'd gone all out with her wedding dress.

Lush ivory satin. Bateau dropped waist. Ruched skirt cascading to the floor. Strapless with a sheer overlay of lace bolero.

She'd loved it on sight.

Looked as if Cinderella had finally got her fairy-tale ending after all.

Along with enough business to keep her busy for the next decade, and a sizable nest egg for Gram, who'd never have another financial worry as long as she lived.

'And I have to say, the job my wife did on this garden?'

He swept his arm wide, encompassing two months' worth of her hard work. 'Not too shabby.'

'Wouldn't want you to be over-effusive with the compliments or anything,' she muttered, playfully whacking him on the chest.

He hauled her to him and the air whooshed out of her lungs. 'I'm saving my compliments for the bedroom tonight. Or this afternoon, if we can get rid of these guests quickly enough.'

She laughed and kissed him on the mouth. 'Still the charmer.'

'Still the most beautiful girl in the world.' He hugged her so tight she could barely breathe.

Not that Lucy cared.

As long as she was in Cash's arms, that was all that mattered.

She might not believe in the romanticism of Valentine's Day, but she sure believed in this wonderful man.

And she would, for the rest of their amazing life together.

Maybe chalk one up to Cupid after all…

* * * * *

ROMANCE

MEDICAL

Mills & Boon® Large Print

February 2014

ROMANCE

HISTORICAL

MEDICAL

Mills & Boon® Hardback
March 2014

ROMANCE

A Prize Beyond Jewels	Carole Mortimer
A Queen for the Taking?	Kate Hewitt
Pretender to the Throne	Maisey Yates
An Exception to His Rule	Lindsay Armstrong
The Sheikh's Last Seduction	Jennie Lucas
Enthralled by Moretti	Cathy Williams
The Woman Sent to Tame Him	Victoria Parker
What a Sicilian Husband Wants	Michelle Smart
Waking Up Pregnant	Mira Lyn Kelly
Holiday with a Stranger	Christy McKellen
The Returning Hero	Soraya Lane
Road Trip With the Eligible Bachelor	Michelle Douglas
Safe in the Tycoon's Arms	Jennifer Faye
Awakened By His Touch	Nikki Logan
The Plus-One Agreement	Charlotte Phillips
For His Eyes Only	Liz Fielding
Uncovering Her Secrets	Amalie Berlin
Unlocking the Doctor's Heart	Susanne Hampton

MEDICAL

Waves of Temptation	Marion Lennox
Risk of a Lifetime	Caroline Anderson
To Play with Fire	Tina Beckett
The Dangers of Dating Dr Carvalho	Tina Beckett

0214GEN STD HB

Mills & Boon® Large Print
March 2014

ROMANCE

Million Dollar Christmas Proposal	Lucy Monroe
A Dangerous Solace	Lucy Ellis
The Consequences of That Night	Jennie Lucas
Secrets of a Powerful Man	Chantelle Shaw
Never Gamble with a Caffarelli	Melanie Milburne
Visconti's Forgotten Heir	Elizabeth Power
A Touch of Temptation	Tara Pammi
A Little Bit of Holiday Magic	Melissa McClone
A Cadence Creek Christmas	Donna Alward
His Until Midnight	Nikki Logan
The One She Was Warned About	Shoma Narayanan

HISTORICAL

Rumours that Ruined a Lady	Marguerite Kaye
The Major's Guarded Heart	Isabelle Goddard
Highland Heiress	Margaret Moore
Paying the Viking's Price	Michelle Styles
The Highlander's Dangerous Temptation	Terri Brisbin

MEDICAL

The Wife He Never Forgot	Anne Fraser
The Lone Wolf's Craving	Tina Beckett
Sheltered by Her Top-Notch Boss	Joanna Neil
Re-awakening His Shy Nurse	Annie Claydon
A Child to Heal Their Hearts	Dianne Drake
Safe in His Hands	Amy Ruttan

Discover more romance at

www.millsandboon.co.uk

- ♥ WIN great prizes in our exclusive competitions

- ♥ BUY new titles before they hit the shops

- ♥ BROWSE new books and REVIEW your favourites

- ♥ SAVE on new books with the Mills & Boon® Bookclub™

- ♥ DISCOVER new authors

PLUS, to chat about your favourite reads, get the latest news and find special offers:

- ▶ Find us on facebook.com/millsandboon
- ▶ Follow us on twitter.com/millsandboonuk
- ♥ Sign up to our newsletter at millsandboon.co.uk